GHOST WRITTEN BY PICARD THE CAT

To Margie

Thanks for the
local support!
God Bless you
and your family

Romans: 5-7

GHOST WRITTEN BY PICARD THE CAT

Donald I. Templeman

iUniverse, Inc.

New York Lincoln Shanghai

GHOST WRITTEN BY PICARD THE CAT

iUniverse books may be ordered through booksellers or by contacting:

iUniverse
2021 Pine Lake Road, Suite 100
Lincoln, NE 68512
www.iuniverse.com
1-800-Authors (1-800-288-4677)

ISBN-13: 978-0-595-36679-8 (pbk)
ISBN-13: 978-0-595-67406-0 (cloth)
ISBN-13: 978-0-595-81101-4 (ebk)
ISBN-10: 0-595-36679-1 (pbk)
ISBN-10: 0-595-67406-2 (cloth)
ISBN-10: 0-595-81101-9 (ebk)

Printed in the United States of America

In loving memory of my best friend, "good and honest" Picard

CONTENTS

▼

FOREWORD

Ghost Written by Picard the Cat? Okay, what's the gimmick? Well truthfully, there is no gimmick here. My friend, Picard the cat, was at my feet (or roaming somewhere about the premises) during the writing of my first two novels and the majority of the short stories contained herein. I won't belabor the heartfelt kinship developed between myself and this wonderful animal during this exciting and creative period of my life. But suffice it to say, I felt it wholly appropriate to dedicate the publication of these short works to my late night typing compatriot who has now moved on to the highest plane of eternal feline spirits.

Up to now, I had been hesitant to release these first person narratives, in part, because they are so brutally effective. That is, the majority of people who have read these stories invariably came back to me saying "wow, you went through a lot!", or "I can't believe you feel that way!", or "I can't believe you did that to her!".

Lost on these enthusiastic readers, is the fact that these are works of FICTION. Fiction, meaning that very little if anything that happens in these stories ever actually occurred. Rather, they are a fusion of perspective and imagination written in the voices of created characters best suited to convey these gripping tales of fun and fantasy.

For the record, I have never been a womanizing misogynist, an angry militant African American college student or…a cat. What I am is a writer who heartily enjoys delving into the inertias and emotions of living souls (more often human than feline) and conjuring up razor sharp characterizations and imagery that impacts each individual reader on a deeply personal level.

When the character in "Under the Store" is chased by a swarming tide of rats, the reader's skin is supposed to crawl with discomfort. When he is confronted by the return of his "deceased" father, the confounding emotions of this reunion are meant to be as darkly disturbing to the guts of the audience as the return of any loved one they have witnessed lowered into their grave.

"The Wisdom of Agnostic Misogyny" is an explosive narrative from the perspective of an amoral young man who has mastered the art of misusing women for his pleasure…yet truthfully finds little pleasure or joy in so doing. With a steady stream of casual sex in ready abundance, what's missing? Love? The agnostic answers are far more complex than that.

Christian perspectives are explored through the adultery of a pastor's wife in "Frailty" and the desire to rescue the soul of a dancer from a gentleman's club in "Lost Mercedes".

Romance unfulfilled is vividly rendered by "The Face of My Son" and "Alena Smiled".

Thought-provoking satire is offered up in the maturation of a double-minded urban college student plunged onto a rural Ohio school campus in the racially charged misadventures of "Tracy X".

And of course, there is the heart-felt reminder "These are Good Days, Picard" from the real author of these works, Picard the cat!

The variations in dialects also enhance the transcendent perspectives. Many of these stories are written in 19th Century archaic Romanticist English even though the settings are clearly modern. Others are written in simpler contemporary dialects that are easily recognized in our 21st Century society.

In the novels I've published thus far, *The Last Champion of Earth* and *The Planet of Mortal Worship*, the focus is clearly upon the relationship between God and man. In these short works, much like Shakespeare and Hawthorne, the focus rests more upon the vulnerabilities and intrigue of the human condition beneath Heaven.

"How now, 'good and honest' Picard?"

We shall certainly see.

—Donald I. Templeman, 2005

FRAILTY

Plummeted to the deepest depth of despair and recrimination, casting hideous aspersions on even the faintest flicker of light that should suggest some remnant of nobility in my "character", I never, even at such moments, considered that I alone could deliver so ghastly a spiritual pestilence to so many as was the case some months ago.

The terrible deed for which I must exonerate all co-conspirators who partook, save myself, dawned on the day I chose to attend a Sunday service at the open invitation of a good friend and co-worker. Having heartily rejoiced in the rare company of dear comrades and loving family for the two days past, something I thought holy at the time, beckoned me to offer thanks to God almighty by means outside the routine of my daily bedside petition. It stood to reason that I could ensure the succession of my merry mood and enhance my strengthening bond with Heaven by counting myself as, at the least, a visitor among my friend's congregation.

Prone to making my own way in many things, I smashed an icy snow drift into a parking space with the bow of my rusted Cavalier, then made my way to the front of a dark brick building that carried no identifiable markings. I stood for a moment and observed several persons entering the glass doors and ascending a flight of carpeted stairs. Unconvinced that I had arrived at the "correct" house of worship, I wandered next door to the undisturbed, decidedly vacant building which carried the sign of my friend's denominational contingent. To the amusement of everyone I pulled the door handles twice and thrice making certain there was no access to be gained and revealed myself as scarcely a regular attendant.

Three-quarters certain that the unmarked building was indeed the church of my good friend, I proceeded up the carpeted stairs toward the swell of gospel rhythms and decided to seek him out. To my dismay no such steadfast confirmation of my whereabouts was forthcoming. As service had already begun, I peered through the door windows and searched the faces of the deacons who stood before the throng (my friend, himself being a deacon) but found him not. Thus, again, attempting to veil my unfamiliarity with my surroundings I casually queried a bystander as to the whereabouts of my friend, mentioning him by name. The bystander then, as I had before, peered through the door windows and searched the pews. After a moment he confirmed to me that my friend was not present but should be, which at least assured me that I had stumbled upon my intended destination.

All things considered I genuinely cared not whether the day carried itself out with precision. This day, mine was a carefree and unburdened lot that simply desired to see the afternoon's proceedings pass thoughtfully and without complication. Such whimsical loftiness was throttled asunder as the lobby doors swung open bidding myself and my fellow latecomers admittance.

She, with her warm, disarming, unavoidably unpretentious, gleaming smile, harmonized with eyes that avowed intelligent feminine gregariousness as royalty wields a scepter, and painted on an unblemished golden canvas by the hand of a peerless artisan, shredded the comfort of my long cherished bachelorhood with a swift and simple greeting.

Would that I had received so fair a hand of fellowship on the day I last exited the church of my grandfather so many years ago. Such an event most certainly would have inspired me to earn my daily bread from the pulpit rather than the desk of indifference at my then, current employ.

Still, noting that I had assigned too much significance to so incidental a meeting, I proceeded to distance myself from the meeting and immersed myself in the service.

I succeeded in this endeavor for all of five minutes. For when the minister instructed everyone to stand in recognition of the entrance of the ladies choir, my recognition immediately re-focused on she who had already unhinged my sensibilities.

As the swaying choir's procession marched down the aisle toward their loft stationed behind the minister, I seized this opportunity to find in her some flaw, some imperfection, that would enable me to dismiss my fixation. Alas, my search for a perceptible shortcoming only confirmed my original cognition which had hastily pedestaled this woman above all I had known previously.

Somewhere betwixt anger, frustration and guilt I resigned myself to the duplicity of my attentions. On the one hand: my friend's Holy service playing out before me like a spiritual symphony of Heavenly worship. On the other hand: my self-serving humanity, recording her every fourth movement, fantasizing of how fate should orchestrate our next chance encounter.

During the opening song, so purposeful were the tides of musical reverberations which washed over us all, that some patrons were moved to outward emotional displays of their embrace of the Holy Spirit. One woman began shouts of joy that culminated with her noteworthy girth collapsing into the arms of waiting ushers whose strength and skill were aptly tested. Another woman from the choir screamed uncontrollably until she deemed the amount of consolation she received sufficient to quell her demonstrative outburst. Even the lead singer, the aforementioned bystander, rode the mounting crest of congregational synergy into several unrehearsed choruses that could have run an hour and still appeared wholly appropriate.

Yet, while moved by all that I observed during this heralding stanza, my cursed mortal consciousness intermittently diverted to my beauteous welcomer who stood devoutly perched behind the minister's left shoulder. Indeed, she too, was overtaken by the heavenly power that surged throughout the church and probably out onto Buckeye Road. But as she closed her eyes and stretched her graceful form skyward, her serene expression was one that carried a deeper and truer understanding of what all of this meant and would mean to both our imperfect ephemeral humanity and our immortal souls before the Throne. From her, there were no screams of anguish or joy. Just a smile and a tear as the warmth of Heaven's light caressed her enviable and undeniable assuredness.

When the music finally flourished to a conclusion and the service appeared ready to settle into the business of bringing our minds in juxtaposition with our hearts, I resolved that I would undivide my attentions with finality. This house of worship, certainly during a service, was no place for me to indulge my male proclivities. It was about that time or shortly thereafter, that my welcomer then stood and took the podium.

Her stint was indeed too lengthy for my crumbling resolve, yet too brief for my dauntless adoration. Ironically, her part was to greet this day's visitors among whom I numbered. True to my nature, I used this interlude to myopically extract her name from the service bulletin. With her "identity" now indelibly etched in my selective memory I could, with greater ease nestle into the day's sermon.

The Minister was, refreshingly, the antithesis of televangelical charlatans who have, over decades, dulled the ears of the masses to the words of God through either overt acts of blatant hypocrisy or the more subtle and more damaging distortions of God's message. His words were ungarnished shards of truth, clearly visible to even those not blessed with a physical sense of sight. And in league with the most gifted of orators, he made hours appear as mere minutes. Thus, before we could tire of him, he tired of us and bid us leave of his service until the following Sunday.

With the many lesions in my faith bandaged for my return to the world of secular pursuits, I briefly crossed paths with my friend's wife who informed me that my friend should be waiting for her outside. Eager to tease him on the matter of my attendance of a service which he, himself had failed to attend, I hurried out the door and found him idled in his vehicle awaiting the emergence of his family.

Stunned beyond words he squinted as if unconvinced that I in fact, stood before him fresh from a Sunday service. I laughed out loud while he continued to shake his head in utter disbelief. Finally a gust of cold winter's breeze drove us back to the refuge of his warming vehicle.

I complimented him on the astounding renovation of the church's inside which starkly contrasted its admittedly rough-hewn exterior. I complimented him on the exuberance and precision of the youthful musicians that accompanied a choir whose virtuosity might have as effortlessly shone singing a cappella. I complimented him on the minister whose raw veracity rekindled in me what I had always enjoyed most about attending such services.

And of course, I complimented him (though in this he had no hand) on the angelic, earthbound, vision of Christian majesty which had greeted me so shortly after my arrival. Though upon naming her to my friend, my impassioned fancy was unceremoniously doused.

"Oh, you mean the minister's wife?" he said in an even tone which commanded my senses back to their vacated reality.

Irony can often be so masterful in the timing of its unveiling, that it should sometimes be forgiven for the indifference of its cruelty.

If my random attendance of this service absented by my friend had been an unintended prank upon him, his singular statement of fact touchéd me threefold.

I hesitated a moment, then could do naught but laugh at my own fool's folly. "The minister's wife" I chuckled to myself. Of this, we proceeded to make light sport until my friend's wife and daughter appeared from behind the church front. I bid my friend adieu and headed home still amazed by my adult predilection for reckless adolescent presumptuousness.

So would that this, up to now, simple tale of a man's three hour infatuation with a woman he never knew, had given up to resting peacefully as one, amid the countless billions of such tales all men living and dead have shared. But as deeply as I tried to bury this wink of time in my years of memory, fate exhumed the story and demanded it continue past the boundaries of its natural life and toward an unsavory after-death which tainted everything in its wake.

Some weeks after the matter had long run its course as a source of amusement, my friend finally invited me to dine at his estate a short distance away. Never one to reject the offer of sustenance without charge I accepted his hospitality with no hesitation. What my friend neglected to tell me, was that the supper would also be attended by the minister and the minister's wife!

My friend's wife welcomed me at the front door and offered me warm conveyance into her home. She took my coat and led me to the dining room where, to my shock, my joy, my consternation sat the minister and his wife. It was fortunate that my mien had already been grafted into a smiling pose. For certainly, confronted with these unforeseen variables, my expression would have been hard-pressed to muster a mask of unfettered neutrality.

I met the minister's firm handshake, offering earnest praise for his message of wisdom at his only service I had attended: The Bible's warnings to be heeded, commandments to be obeyed, facts to be believed, and promises to be realized. I then held the delicate fingers of the minister's wife, feigning scant recollection of our previous meeting. In this moment, it was to my horror I discovered that my knowledge of her wedded covenant failed miserably to abate my amorous affections.

When my friend finally entered the room, having beaten back his latest domestic adversary with hammer and nail, we randomly seated ourselves to the table. As the odd member, I chose my seat toward the middle of the table in an attempt to position my straying conscience to a least offending location. My friend and the minister chose opposite heads of the red clothed table. Their wives settled cater-cornered to their lefts. Needless to say, I was further shaken as the coincidence of our arrangement placed the minister's wife directly across the way.

The minister blessed the meal to which we were about to receive and as delectable dishes were passed from place to place, the evening settled into casual conversation most of which focused upon an Easter program that was in its preliminary planning stages. A great deal was made of who desired to fill what role and who was best suited to perform what role. The chasm twixt "desired" and "suited" served as the impetus for biting humorous levity from the wife of my friend and was accented by the calm, illuminating candor of the minister's wife.

Promptly, my hedonistic guile seized the dialogue as an opportunity to muse in the song of her melodic voice and revel in the flicker of candlelight which brightly embellished the portrait of her soft, porcelain crafted features. For those seconds I found myself unable to dam the rush of my thoughts, so I painlessly relented to their engulfing flood.

Only my friend's mention of my name broke the timeless trance. He'd suggested a small speaking part for my voice in the aforementioned program, which best suited my talents. They all, then, commented on the resonance of its tone, but it was the merely obligatory compliment from the minister's wife which I took deludingly to heart.

The balance of the dinner conversation lightheartedly poked about my friend's elusive quest to sire a son, he having already been the producer two healthy young daughters. That, and how myself, a gentleman bearing no visible disfigurements, had thus far evaded the bond, or chains, if you will, of marital "bliss". As the minister took up the opportunity to facetiously lecture me on the absence of virtue my evasion of obligation carried, my friend's wife followed, playfully concluding that I was obviously the type of narcissist who valued the company of himself more than he could ever value that of a woman. At that, the minister's wife offered me silent condolence with her eyes as a pre-adolescent would tease another under bullied siege on a rain soaked school yard.

Thankfully, my friend, having some knowledge of my wick's end on the belaboring of this topic, rose from the table and suggested we all adjourn to the living room.

I could not help but watch how without overbearance, the minister lovingly escorted his wife toward the next room. His movements were not at all practiced, but guided by a genuine warmth, undiminished by the trials of holy matrimony. At that instant I concluded that any force of nature or otherwise, which sought to intercede its will on so well set a couple, could only be born of a devilish hell-spawned lust, bent to consume its misguided victims.

And so it was.

The telephone rang and hastily my friend's wife called the minister to the phone. It seemed that a recently emancipated convict, new to the church's fellowship, had found assimilation into civilian life more burdensome than ever imagined. He promised the minister to engage in some drastic measure harmful to at least himself this night lest the minister met with him anon.

So with dutiful haste, the minister took up his hat and coat, and bidding his wife to remain, bid us all a "good eve".

As the headlights of the minister's vehicle rolled through the front curtains, my friend's wife speculated on what matter could bring the ex-convict to so desperate a circumstance so soon after his release. The minister's wife speculated further, citing the hardships of attempting to re-insert one's self into our cruel, aloof and desolately uncaring society. My friend then put in that the convict, well built and still youthful, should take up the trade of professional pugilism noting that a renowned pugilist had recently been made a convict by recent judicial proceedings. With that, the evening's mood again lightened and conversation eddied to recent newsworthy events.

My friend's wife broached the topic of men who covertly impose their passions on women in the place of their mutual employ. And moreover, what a woman should do in the event that the man who so imposes is also her direct superior.

Seated on the outskirts of the room, the safest haven for my smouldering vacillations, my fading reason sought to rescue me from the indulgence of my fantasies by advocating a boorish, anti-feminine posture during the discussions, rendering any opinion the minister's wife might have of me, tolerable but scarcely desirable.

It was in the hours that followed that I overturned my verdict on the alleged female predilection for total unpredictability which, up to now, I had ascribed to the prattlings of lesser men than myself.

When my friend's wife suggested that men are inherently libidinous lechers who utilize the workplace to satiate their voyeuristic appetites, I professed that it was the irresponsible exhibitionism of women that made men so.

To the utterance of this intentionally slanted posture, I fully expected the minister's wife to reprimand me with a cordial tongue lashing for harboring so obstinately biased an opinion. But, to my surprise, she merely smiled and acknowledged that women are not totally without blame under such circumstances and that both sides should work together to ensure that sexual signals, transmitted or received in a professional environment, be held to a minimum. She then complimented me on my adept wielding of paradoxical sarcasm to route the topic toward a viable resolution.

Undaunted by my initial failure to discredit my structure of values, I continued, at each opportunity, to espouse philosophies that would have sent any good Christian searching for the nearest fire arm. To this end I cannot say that I was totally unsuccessful in stirring discontent. Regretfully, by evening's end those ill-feelings were erroneously aroused in my friend's wife, who, as I now recollect, ne'er spoke to me thereafter. My friend, while not angered, was perplexed by my behavior. And the minister's wife...well...enjoyed herself immensely citing my intelligent, dichotomous wit as unrivaled amongst her vast and varied associations.

I had always bemoaned that my attempts to display charm and intellect to the women I desired fell unnoticed. This night, I found on equal footing, my inability dismantle my credibility in the face of a woman from whom common decency demanded I withhold more than obligatory amenities.

With the evening at an end, and my manipulations of perceptions in shambles I snapped on my coat, longing for the asylum of my unfretted abode. For I had had my fill of having dangled before me that which would and should be ever denied me.

But before I could expedite my escape, I overheard my friend's wife attempting to convince the minister's wife not to walk home alone. The minister's wife suggested that it was only a short distance but my friend's wife insisted that it was too late an hour for her to travel unescorted. Finally my friend, rarely putting himself ahead of what is best, offered her conveyance home.

I was deafened by my own silence. Were I not departing also? What possible inconvenience could it be to assure the minister's wife safe passage? None at all. Yet the guilt over my duplicity of purpose was deafening as well. Her, alone with me: A pathetically depraved, yet wonderfully appealing prospect. And so under guise of being the good samaritan, I insistently pronounced that conveying the minister's wife home would be no trouble to me at all.

She alighted on the passenger's seat and searched in the darkness for the safety belt. I started the motor, then reached across her to secure the belt she could not find, again questioning whether my dueling motives were only offering assistance.

Wrestling to remain in the role of chauffeur, her soothing voice and her previously undetectable alluring scent filled the moving vehicle. Between offering direction, she probed immediately into the heart of my curious behavior during our evening's discussions.

It was not enough that she did not accept my alignment with absurdity at face value as had, unfortunately, my friend's wife. She had also not believed that my attempts at self-defamation were merely satirically comedic interjections. She knew it was something more. And in spite of my outwardly indivisible attentions toward everyone, she knew it had to do with her.

"You don't like me, do you?" she said with confounded innocence. The inaccuracy of this polarized suggestion commanded my jaw to set despite my sincerest hope to remain sternly inscrutable. She interpreted that subtle gesture as affirmation of her painfully errant claim and with a sigh settled back.

I was altruistically content to allow her accusation to stand rather than even hint at my ashamed affections in her favor. I was not unlike a creature denizened in Pandora's box, fighting to keep the lid sealed from within. Would that Pandora herself had been so wise, for her strength prevailed that day, unleashing a tide of iniquity that rotted all that stood in its path.

And so it was.

As we pulled in front of the minister's house, I could feel the eyes of the minister's wife searching me for some satisfactory rebuttal to her charges. I strained to remain impassive. To this she, in spite of myself, cordially responded by expressing gladness at having met someone who carried in him a unique air of poorly concealed nobility and decency even if he saw none of that in her. She concluded with the hope that whatever I found lacking in her would be no reflection on my friend or her husband's ministry.

This final gesture of selfless grace annihilated the good sense of my disintegrating resolve.

As she swung around to disembark from the vehicle I, as gently as possible, grasped her wrist causing her to turn back. Absent of fair warning, I lunged across the passenger side and blindly kissed her on her cheek.

She met my eyes with total confusion. Then shook her head, smiled warmly, and slammed the door shut.

That night, I cursed myself to sleep with every profane castigation I could muster for elevating my empty earth-bound longings above the sanctity of the minister's wife.

The next week, I avoided meeting the gaze of my friend for fear he might recognize the admission of deviant criminality in my eyes. Although, for all I could know the minister's wife had already related my warrantless action causing my friend to purposely alienate my corrupted presence.

In either case I neither slept nor ate for seven days, relentlessly harassed by my monumental indiscretion. Finally, I reasoned that the only absolution on Earth that could be given would not be given by me, but by the minister's wife herself.

Sunday, before daylight, I arrived at my friend's church and sat still, in waiting for the arrival of the minister and his wife. A half-hour later they did appear, and it only then, dawned on me that they might remain inseparable for the better part of the day. But as fortune, as I chose to acknowledge it, would have it, she reappeared moments later, alone in the parking lot opening the trunk of her burgundy Bonneville.

More stealthily than intended I came upon her from behind giving her an unsettling start. As she turned, her face flashed a momentary panic at my decidedly frightful appearance. But as I spoke, her countenance melted into relieved recognition.

After apologizing for surprising her thusly, I further apologized for my inexcusably sophomoric churlishness the Saturday before last. I confessed that I was rarely prone to such acts and that yes, her beauty had inspired in me the poorest judg ment. I vowed ne'er to haunt her or hers again with my troubling and disturbed presence and having said all of this, attempted to depart, my truth made known.

But the minister's wife spoke, and the tune commanded me to listen. She offered that my action was received as no less than mere flattery…and no more. She advised against further self-persecution citing that my denial of any earnest feelings in this matter would be criminal to my humanity and any proponent of truth therein.

She, in fact, beckoned me to stay for morning service but I declined noting that I was grossly unaccoutered and ungroomed for the occasion.

Finally, with the cord nearly cut and my soul nearly whole, she scribed a number on a square of paper where she could be reached if I required further counsel on the matter. As I took the number in hand, a portion of me rejoiced that some linkage would remain. A wiser portion of my soul, however, lamented at what might yet come of it.

Normally proficient in dissociating myself from situations potentially iniquitous, I grappled poorly with the logic of either retaining or destroying the number the minister's wife had given me.

"I could call her under pretense of needing counsel," I thought, "but God would recognize the pretense full well and hold me accountable. But what pretense? Am I not truly in need of further counsel? And who better than the minister's wife to assure me that no transgression was manifested in my moment of weakness?"

This unbalanced extrapolation continued for eleven days. On the seventh day I was certain that rationality had prevailed when I conclusively crumpled the dreaded paper and tossed it into a public receptacle. But on the eighth day I found that while the paper had been disposed, the number had been committed to memory. Helplessly, I made the inevitable phone call on a fateful Thursday afternoon.

Details of what followed need not be recounted here. For I have suffered through the remembrance of that long coveted, depraved evening which forever maimed the faith and souls of so many, every waking moment since its passing. To this day I know not whether the minister's wife came to my spartan dwelling that thankless night purely predisposed to genuinely assisting a bewildered lamb strayed from the flock. Or whether she came readily prepared to be lured from the narrow path and into complicity with a wolf's dark amoral decadence. I am only certain that all I had admired in her, I murdered that horrific evening.

In the days that followed, I attempted to console myself since I'd discovered myself unsuitable to be consoled by others. Failing even in this, I sought refuge in the only teachings I believed could offer me salvation. But found only that in willing the events which orchestrated adultery, I was the most condemned and wretched creature of all.

The scope of the plague I did wrought was made known to me after some months. In casual conversation with my friend, I learned that the congregation had fallen on difficult times. For you see, the minister had confided to my friend that the faith which empowered his preachings had been shaken by his certain contention that the fidelity of the minister's wife had been compromised. And while she insistently denied any such unholy transgression, he could see it plainly in the eyes which could no longer hold his own. With Satan's malevolent reign visited upon his personal dominion, the minister found himself desperately under siege and not wholly adequate to provide leadership to those most in need.

My friend had advised him to continue on, but verily, the earnest sting of the minister's whip was lost in the malaise of the minister's vulnerable humanity. And the biting fervor which had drawn thousands into the congregation for years, now, in its absence, crumbled away the faithful with sedate, dutiful, uninspired sermons. Indeed, the diminished spirituality which pervaded each passing Sunday caused even a tiny rift between my friend and his wife, occasioning him to seek refuge in my company at a local tavern.

Upon the hearing of this, the shame of my treachery forbade me from sharing my knowledge of the truth. Still, I groped for the one decent act that might undo the sin I could never undo in the eyes of God.

On the next Sunday, I resolved to return to the site where I had first been overtaken by the visage of the minister's wife. There, I would confess my crime before the church and lay waste to the sickness deceit had visited upon them all. And whatever merciless punishment awaited me I cared not. For in the absence of truth made manifest, my very existence carried with it no meaning at all.

And so with dread for how the truth would, in the short term, affect the congregation and my friend and my friend's wife and the minister and the minister's wife, I plodded the carpeted stairs following the now listless music which had been unwittingly sapped by my foul deed.

As I entered the pews, I shuddered at the sight of litter and spillage from weeks past, left unpoliced by those now shackled by the chains of their indifference. Attendance was only half of what I had seen previously.

I cringed at the sound of the minister's wavering cracked voice and the sight of the gray mask he wore as his face.

My heart sank at the sagging sight of my friend standing as a deacon, his collar undone, his face unshaven, (for verily we did imbibe heavily the night just past), and his family nowhere to be seen.

But none of this moved me to the precipice of tears as did the crumpled apparition which scarcely resembled the minister's wife. The eyes which had enraptured me months before were now dim and swollen from months of unslumbered melancholia. Her once, silken mane was pinned eschew, jutting straw-like about her head. The bright glow of her complexion was replaced by a drawn and jaundiced hue painfully punctuated by her weight which had diminished a third.

This garish nightmare is what sprung up from the seeds planted by my wanton avarice. More than any thief, nay any devil could have hoped, I had destroyed from within that which God had intended to last an eternity!

With no hope for myself, I prayed that the devastation sprawled before me could be reconciled. And with nothing to lose, when the minister did beckon members of the waning faithful to ask petition, I did stand to speak my horrid truth.

But before I could utter a sound, the minister's wife, upon eyeing my presence and perhaps my intent, collapsed into the loft unable to bear up any longer under the burden of the unspoken crime.

I ran to the front fearing the worst was yet to pass. When I arrived, the minister was already kneeling at her side. My friend knelt forward offering her a chalice of water.

I stooped down beside the minister and watched as the parched lips of the minister's wife were resurrected by the cool sustenance. She tried to speak aloud but the minister forbid it.

I looked at the minister and he met my eyes with a vindictive scowl. I turned to my friend who returned to me an admonishing frown. I stood and looked out over the pews and gauged a mounting hostility.

With resignation, I met no other stares of disapproval and departed from the shells my wretched sickness left stricken.

finis

UNDER THE STORE

"Alive!" was the word I shouted into the dark stillness as the cool perspiration which coated my flesh shrieked threats to hurl my newly discovered awareness into frozen, catatonic shock.

Every muscle in my body tightened. Tendons tore from bone. I could feel my crawling scalp ripping away from my skull as the veins in my temples, my jaws and my neck set to burst, stressed beyond their capacity to convey blood.

Only a subconscious vault from the bed into the sharp edge my dresser dislodged the knotted bondage with which my body had nearly choked off my last breath.

As my rebellious sinews ached back to their former lodgings, my memory was finally graced the luxury of capsulizing its nightmared recollections: The store. The shattered glass beneath my feet. The smell of cigarettes, wine and expired medicines. The sound of a scratched Blue Note jazz album. And the sight of the old man…nestled comfortably amidst the wreckage!

I sat up naked on the cold wooden floor and felt my limbs tingle back from their rigored slumber. I breathed my first, albeit bloody and rasped, breath in what seemed like hours. Then I quivered a smile as the pain of life was a welcomed comfort, having just clawed myself from the hellish sphere of desolate irrevocable lifelessness.

I carefully hoisted my bulk to the cracking of my legs onto feet that felt as if insects danced inside their soles. I leaned over into the mirror and searched through swollen, pulsing orbs for my identity.

Haggard though the visage was, it was clearly "me". Though the thought flashed across my mind wondering why I didn't have a beard.

"We're all here." I smirked and then stretched, taking inventory of the resurrected muscle.

Satisfied with my self-inspection, I began the routine of plotting the day's course when all at once, I was besieged by the urgency of locating the time. My clearing eyes skirted the walls and surfaces and shortly found a large LED read-out displaying a bright red "4:50 am".

I might have been gone a week or a month for all I knew. I peered out of a window and snow still dusted the earth. But this confirmed only that at the least, Spring had not yet broken. I stroked my face to gauge whisker growth, but there wasn't enough to justify even the time I knew had passed. Finally, the thought dawned on me to punch on the television and dial up the annoying cable scroll that carried a running synopsis of the current time, temperature and date.

Cathode ray-light enveloped the living room accompanied by a deafening garble that painfully rebirthed my hearing. Hastily flipping through the channels I located the monotonous scroll accompanied by a dreary radio simulcast. The time was now "4:52". The temperature was 27 degrees. The date was December 28.

It was only tomorrow. What else should it be?

Comforted by the disclosure of "when", I sat down on the cracked vinyl couch and recounted the last twenty-four hours, which had forever skinned away my familiar identity and replaced it with a fresh obsession of singular purpose.

Actually, the first hour of the last twenty-four had been a culmination of years of what I thought had been futile speculation. For you see, from the very hour that my father's death had been pronounced, some part of me, void of mournful longing, sensed that his passing was little more than an elaborate ruse orchestrated solely to relieve him of the tortured asphyxiation his life had become.

Having single-handedly thrown off the shackles of oppressive poverty and innate societal bigotry, he degreed himself at a local university and promptly bolted the netherworld of the inner-city never again to be plagued by its cycle of self-inflicted despair indigenous to its trifled boulevards.

He prospered well, he married well, he sired well and he generally lived well. But to his consternation, the lingering stench of his less than modest origin could never be bathed from his permeated flesh.

In prosperity, as a licensed apothecary, he succeeded well for a time. However the times themselves were unkind to the profession as the recreational misuse of pharmaceuticals became the unlawful pursuit of criminal businessmen. And the pressure to illegitimize legitimate men of the trade became insurmountable. All of this, was of course compounded by those of similarly modest origins (and therein destined to remain), who impressed upon him the need to give (with great emphasis on "give") any and all that he could "afford" for the sake of "brotherhood". As my mother so aptly put it, "he played Jesus to the thankless jackals" and for his graciousness was rewarded with abject ruination.

In marriage he succeeded where many fail, finding intelligence, strength, beauty and unquestioned fidelity as the traits of his chosen mate. But the spoils of his wedded coup were weighty and complex. As is often a man's lot, his Herculean successes were met with glancing feminine indifference, while his failures and shortcomings, varied but no more frequent, were underscored with scathing castigation. His pursuit of female perfection had thus, rendered him victim to the perfectionist. His love for her and his amplified sense of self-inadequacy wrestled unabated.

In siring he succeeded, (though, do not interpret this as vanity on my part for surely that is not the intent), creating a diluted reflection of himself that he admired greatly. Yet, having been the product of a fatherless home, he found the role of father more cumbersome than he ever imagined. The balance of when to play, when to teach, when to discipline, when to coddle (mysteries to even the most learned of parents), were like an oiled playing surface, tauntingly cruel to his daunted footing. The "certainty" of imminent failure in this duty often left him to the vices of indecision and avoidance.

In living well he succeeded as king of his castle with all matters of import delegated to the queen. Within his throne room, better known as "the den", he surrounded himself with literature and music and television and liquor and cigarettes enough to sustain a small community, though actual food seemed to always be a sparse commodity. But even these luxuries became excesses, perhaps born of the prosperity, marriage and fatherhood which tightened as a noose about his neck. Verily, in the matter of living well, he treated life as if it scarcely mattered at all.

And so on the evening he departed, it seemed a fitting departure. To leave behind the frustrations and miscues of that first turn at life and embark anew upon fresh waters.

Mind you, even at such a tender age my intellect was sufficient to comprehend death's finality. People died all the time. That someone so close to me should die so untimely was just a matter odds, for I knew that we all returned to the earth sooner or later. His death could not be unlike any other. Indeed, the privilege of being the son of the deceased allowed me to touch the cold, hardened skin, the still soft mustache. By my own account, whatever lay in the casket that day appeared quite dead.

Of course, in the years that followed, there were dreams. There was one of him speaking to a large throng from behind a podium. There was one of him opening up a new store, the shelves stocked with homemade remedies and space aged hardwares and gadgetries. And there were several wherein he moved about the house as if he had never gone and we accepted his non-departure with total normality. And just as matter-of-factly, each morning would wash away the dreamscapes and reality would settle in very comfortably.

But then the sightings began.

The first occurred four years after his passing in a downtown arcade. After school, a friend and I took the train into the city to frequent our favorite comic shoppe. We had just made our purchases and absconded with several unpurchased, when across the avenue I saw as plainly as I could determine, my father in a long black coat loitering carelessly outside of a restaurant. He dropped a cigarette onto the curb, doused it with his foot and turned to enter the establishment. After a stunned hesitation, I bolted through moving and perturbed traffic to catch up to him leaving my puzzled comrade behind. I hurled the door open, burst into the lounge, and saw him sitting at the bar, reaching into his hip pocket for his wallet. As I purposefully strode to confront him, I was intercepted from the blindside by a muscular and uncompromising attendant who needn't have reminded me that I was not yet of drinking age. I begged the brute to simply allow me to speak to the man at the bar. But before my plea was fully spoken I found myself back on the sidewalk staring at my wafting reflection in the closing glass door. Determined to resolve my father's mysterious return, I stood outside the restaurant awaiting his emergence. Couples and foursomes and odd numbered parties came and went, but never did my father exit. Finally, I hid behind another group of entrants and stole back into the lounge only to find that where he once sat lay broken nut shells, an empty glass and several cigarette butts littering an ashtray. Before I could query the bartender, the attendant was upon me again and this time I left on my own accord. I never spoke of that afternoon to anyone and over time was even able to ascribe it to mistaken identity.

But a few years later, I saw him again. I was riding the bus to the terminal after a day at my summer employ. I sat lazily peering out of the window when suddenly I saw him trot down a flight of stairs in front of a church and duck into a waiting taxi. It was not just his face I recognized, but his heavy legged, staccato gait. I interrogated my senses to determine whether it was an illusion or trick of the eye. As plain as my fingers dug into my seat, it was him! My bus, however, continued on before I could react. Behind us I could see the taxi turn down a sidestreet and my father was again, shuffled back into the megalopolitan deck.

That same summer, I saw him once more, leisurely window shopping behind a television reporter's shoulder as I sat in my bedroom. Two years later, I saw him enter a jazz concert and spent the better part of an hour and a half searching the faces of enthusiasts for his visage. And a year and a half ago, I certainly saw him leaving a liquor store and quickly vanishing around a nearby corner.

Of course amidst these true sightings were a number of false ones. I had seen a man who bore his resemblance with a younger family at an amusement park. But upon closer examination, the man was too tall and too young. I had also inaccurately sighted him outside a mission among the destitute, but this too proved to be false. Countless times, having known that I had seen him, I began to see him where he was not.

Finally, for the sake of my teetering sanity on this matter, I resolved that they had all been misjudgments on my part and I would no longer entertain absurd notions that he still dwelled among the breathing. Since the day of his "death" other family members I had been closer to had passed on, and I ne'er once saw their twins, their ghosts or even an animal reincarnation ambling about thereafter. There was no rational reason why such behavior regarding my father should persist.

Then, there was yesterday.

Driving home from work I became trapped by the holiday traffic behind a city bus, the mastodons of boulevard congestion. Navigation of the roads was treacherous due to the tall rows of brown slush that bordered each lane. Unable free myself of the binding wet track I relented to my fate behind the mammoth public transport.

The bus carelessly wafted its massive husk between the outer edges of our lane and the uneven edges of the curbs like a near mindless pachyderm: singular in its purpose and certain that no meaningful harm could be done by those beneath it.

Imprisoned in the cockpit of my vehicle I used the frequent stops to observe people in their varied holiday moods. As always there were the children, underdressed for the climate and overexuberant for the adults around them. Two boys, about the age of nine chased each other around a bus stop and crashed into the protruding backside of a lumbering elderly lady who was already having ample difficulty hoisting her woolen layered girth onto the waiting transport. She snapped her head backwards like an angry condor and glared at the two youths as if she would devour them on the spot. They returned her glare with puppy eyed apologies. As she then continued her labored ascent onto the bus, the boys looked at each other and laughed playfully to one another.

At the next stop was a tall, dark, bony, man clad in a black leather jacket and cap. His eyes were yellow and red rimmed. His beard was scraggly and ungroomed. A cigarette hung from his dark purple lips. A newspaper was crumpled under his armpit. And a worn and tattered transfer dangled in his filthy taloned fingers. His face was the mask of comfortable destitution. For him, it was to be another holiday season that reminded him of all the material items which life had failed to deliver at his feet. He muttered obscene profanity at the smiling teenage girls in front of him as he boarded the bus. Through the back window, I saw the man engage the driver in a decidedly disagreeable conversation. A moment later he dropped out of the bus door, tossed the invalid transfer into the gutter and began swaggering up the street as the bus left him cursing amidst the gray exhaust.

The bus tottered its way to the next stop and unceremoniously swung over to a right turn lane that would finally allow me the freedom to pass. My first welcomed sensation of early evening relief swept over me. But as I accelerated, I saw a man in a long dark coat with a large shopping bag step out of the bus stop. I caught only a glimpse of him, but the instant recognition demanded me to press heavily on my brake for a fuller, affirming view. I glared long and hard into his face as the man, dismayed by my attentions, looked back at me...and knew who I was.

It was him.

Not a ghostly astral apparition; not a conjured surrealist's illusion; not a despair induced vision clouding my sanity! This was the old man, as real as the ridged wheel clutched in my palms, boarding a bus 19 years after he had been pronounced dead.

A car behind me honked its horn. I tried to ease back to my former slot behind the bus, but its misery was inherited by another vehicle in no hurry to fall farther behind.

The bus turned right and an unyielding line followed its trail. The car behind me honked its annoyance again and I was forced to continue straight ahead or face the wrath it and countless other commuting minions would bring down upon me. I reasoned that I could turn at the end of the next block and navigate back to the bus route without losing a large measure of time. Rush hour congestion, however, made the maneuver more difficult.

Speeding down a sidestreet, I narrowly missed crushing a man who mindlessly shoved open his car door and wandered aimlessly into traffic. At the last moment

I swung my car up onto a tree lawn to avoid him then guided it back on to the road. In my mirror I could see the man continuing his trek as if unaware of his near fatality.

I sped to the nearest intersection which intersected with the bus route. I sat at a traffic signal as the bus thundered past. When the light changed, I left turned in front of traffic so as not to lose pace. Then fate set me back again!

A police siren sounded behind me. I pulled over to the side of the road in hope that it would pass my vehicle in pursuit of something less benign. Unfortunately, as I came to a halt against the curb, the police car followed suit.

I cursed loudly behind the muffling of my car's windows. Then spent twenty minutes being lectured on the dangers of reckless operation by an officer who'd better have served the community rousting the teenage drug mongers whose blood-soaked profits rendered the inner avenues barely habitable.

I visually made two narcotics arrests while the paunchy disheveled "lawman" wrote up the citation for my pernicious moving violation. And though my afternoon was now sufficiently destroyed, the act of public servitude seemed to have, at least, done the policeman a good turn as he proudly waggled back to his warm squad car and the pastry box smeared against the inside of its grimy windshield. With a hearty "hi-ho silver" the policeman sounded his siren, hung an illegal u-turn into oncoming traffic then slung his law enforcement vehicle into the drive-thru line of a local fried chicken stand.

With my worst fears of the competence of inner city law enforcement confirmed and my father or his twin or his ghost long out of reach, I pulled on my headlights and plotted my course for home.

Just as I began moving forward, however, another bus rumbled by. It stopped directly in front of me, dispatching several passengers, then continued on its way. The thought then came to me that if it was indeed, my father whom I saw boarding the bus earlier, the slight chance that he was domiciled somewhere along this bus route was worth investigating. So I humored my fool's fancy and followed the bus from station to station.

It might have proved tedious tailing the slow moving behemoth were it not for the fact that the surroundings became increasingly familiar as we traveled east. The Clark gas station I remembered as a child was now a Goodyear service center. The rundown strip stores I hadn't seen in twenty years were now renovated into a modern, albeit low-rent, shopping plaza. The Lawson's where I'd purchased my first and last carbonated chocolate soda was now a hair products outlet. And nothing yet, occupied the Veiner Schnitzel hot dog restaurant which had closed its aluminum spired doors over a decade ago.

The bus tottered on further and I noted the "new" McDonalds which actually wasn't so new anymore. And finally, the tan bricked shopping center with the barber shop, the Red Onion Grille, and the soaped windows of an auto parts store…where the old man's pharmacy once teemed with hopes and dreams.

A marveling "Huh." was all the understatement I could muster.

My cessation of trailing the bus passed subconsciously. I became fixated on the pitted, pollution stained storefront that seemed to sag in remorse over its forsaken vacancy.

My vehicle swayed and bobbed as it entered the brown slushed, pot-holed parking lot. And even through the car windows, the seasoned aroma of the Red Onion's deep fried oils impaled my nostrils.

I pulled in front of a row of cracked, tilted, yellow and gray stalagmites which once served as parking posts guarding the entrance to the old man's store. I cut the engine, cut the lights, and stepped out of the car.

A hazy night sky had now fully enveloped the eve. The sound of dwindling work traffic droned on in the background as I walked slowly toward the card-boarded glass front door. I reached for the door handle fully expecting it to be locked tight. But before my gloved fingers could make certain of this, the silence was startled by loud laughter.

I looked up sharply and saw a large grinning bearded man with a grease stained brown shopping bag, swagger out of the Red Onion two storefronts to my left. As he hefted dinner onto the passenger side of his putty and sanded van, a shorter older man in a dirty white apron (the proprietor, I surmised) appeared outside the doorway.

"Ay, tell your wife if she needs a real man, to give me a call and I'll swing by!" yelled the man in the apron followed by a guttural phlegm impeded chuckle.

"Yeah," responded the bearded man from inside his van. "Just bring your gun!"

They both then laughed loudly again, seemingly to determine who could laugh loudest, as the van's unmuffled engine belched up a start. The van pulled away and the man in the apron, noticed me for the first time. His face sank to a forbidding scowl.

"Nobody's there." he said evenly, in a tone that carried either a statement of the obvious, or a warning to be heeded.

"I know." I said with annoyance, beckoning the man to go back from where he had come.

"Then whatcha' lookin' for?" he persisted.

"I've been trying to catch up with the guy who used to own this place." I hedged.

"Oh, he owes you too?" presumed the man in the apron, referring to the owner of the auto parts store.

"Yeah…big time." I answered, never fully acknowledging the man's presence.

"Well if you find 'im, tell 'im I got somethin' for his ass!" chuckled the man in the apron.

"Hey, I heard you do some serious burgers!" I lied.

"Yeah?" responded the man with shocking gullibility.

"Yeah. Why don't you fire me up a couple and I'll be in there in a minute!"

"It'll be about twenty minutes!" he said with all the professional pride he could muster.

"That'll be just about right."

Mercifully, the man in the apron shuffled back to his purveyance of botulism.

I again reached for the scarred door handles. The metal was stinging cold even through the insulation of my leather ski gloves. I gave a stout tug and the doors lurched forward, then tightened back to their moorings. I pulled again, with greater alacrity but the doors' response was identical, only this time accompanied with the sound of a chain slapping against the interior.

My curiosity unsatiated, I turned and began trudging to the rear of the store. The side wall, facing south, was remarkably uncorroded compared to the rest of the building. Probably due to the fact that it faced away from the northern wind that carried the city's wastes southerly into this now blighted business district. But unmarred, it was not, for its surface had been adopted as a bulletin board for the scribings of delinquent adolescents who now overpopulated the urban avenues. Purported and projected conquests of females sexually and rivals violently were the dominant themes confirming that the prevailing economic inequities were surpassed only by the rotted moral iniquities.

I moved to the rear of the building, and suddenly the world was soundless. Soundless except for the anguished howl of the winter evening's breeze that moaned through the alleyway adjacent to the back of the mall strip. The noise of the traffic to the front of the stores was no longer perceptible.

The rear exits of the strip were almost uniform in their foreboding rusted diligence. Some carried signs. Some carried torn signs. And some, like the store of the old man's carried none. Each exit also neighbored a kindred iron refuse receptacle yawning skyward, receiving indiscriminately anything that might fall from above. With my next movement my senses were accosted by the collectively unbearable pungent, squalid stench of molded meats and soured dairy emanating from the Red Onion's rear.

I covered my face to deaden the putrid odor and stepped quietly, in my mind, attempting not to ripple to life the unseen, indigenous vermin that doubtless frolicked amidst the tactless filth.

Suddenly, the hiss and scream of a feline was followed by its motion, bolting from behind the dumpster one door down from the old man's store. Nipping savagely at its fleeing pads was a gang of four or five rats, each the cat's equal in mass. Two of the gargantuan rodents managed to topple the feline as would a pair of hungry wolves tracking a caribou on the Asian tundra. But the cat managed to roll back to its feet, darting away from the mangy assailants and scurrying up the side of a chain linked fence leaving clumps of bloodied fur in its wake.

The cat then, turned and gave one last spiteful hiss to his attackers. To this, one of the rats responded by charging headlong into the fence and bouncing off screeching ruefully at the feline's narrow escape. Two of his brethren followed. Decisively bested in battle and rhetoric, the cat hobbled away leaving a red and yellow trail in the dirty snow.

In almost military unison, the rats returned to their dumpster, never once noting my presence. As they disappeared under the receptacle, I again heard the shriek of feline agony.

Curious beyond good sense, I walked quietly toward the dumpster until the moonlight was adequate enough to expose a second feline being eaten alive by six or seven rodent captors. The cat's cries were sufficient to chill my blood, but the efficient snapping of small bone and the ripping of flesh left me amazed with disgust. As one rodent carnivore tore away a foreleg for its share, I decided then, that I had witnessed enough.

But as I turned to leave the wretched alleyway I found myself confronted by a black rolling sea of giant rodents flowing from out of the old man's dumpster and trotting towards me!

I cursed out loud and turned back to see the opposing concrete shore also disintegrating under a second tide of rodent warriors.

Like the cat before me, I was now left with a hastened flight up the side of the fence as my only option. I turned and ran toward the fence and could hear the surge of two scampering rodent battalions converging on my position.

I could feel three or four of them on the backs of my legs and coat as I jumped onto the fence and climbed faster than I could have imagined. I felt sharp pains in my calves as blended wool served poorly for protection from the vermin horde.

Still, momentary relief crept over me as I reached the top of the fence. But relief was short lived as I managed to skewer my hand on the steel spikes protruding from the top.

All at once, my dilemma exponentially worsened as I had to carefully and painfully remove my hand from the fence while rats chewed away on my neck and legs.

As I struggled to free my hand, I heard human shouting from behind. In another moment, I felt something swishing against my back that, with each pass, swept the miscreant hybrids from my clothing.

When I was sure that no rodent sat on my shoulder waiting to pluck out my eye, I peaked backward and saw a tall, gaunt figure fanatically waving a broom. Beyond the figure, I could see the rodent armies in full retreat, returning to their iron bunkers.

I was not fully prepared to trust anyone after so harrowing an encounter, and my first reflex was to leap from the fence burying my foot in the figure's chest. The man, so effective in combating rats toppled clumsily into a puddle of slush!

He looked up at me, and began to laugh. "You used to kick me jus' like that when you was a little kid." he cackled in broken dialect.

"Who the hell are you?" I queried between short breaths.

"Al!" said the man as he uncoiled his gangly frame from the ground.

"Al." I muttered to myself searching my memory for old acquaintances by that name.

"Yeah, Al!" clarified the man. "Your old man's stock boy!"

I immediately remembered the tall skinny teenager my father employed a quarter of a century ago. However this man was a haggard, tight-skinned, watery eyed skeleton of the young man I had known then. But something, most likely, his knowledge of the name of the old man's stock boy coupled with his recognition of me, told me that this rat-mastering rescuer was exactly who he claimed to be.

The words that followed were even more surprising. He turned and headed for the back door.

"Well, you comin'? He's still open."

With that, Al disappeared behind the rusted iron entrance.

"Still open?" I questioned the air. "That's ridic..."

The door slapped shut against the door frame severing my thought from its analysis of the absurd. It was like awakening in the midst of a dream as all at once everything that even hinted at the presence of Al, or the rats, save the sting of my bleeding hand, had vanished.

Eager not to lose my link with preceding events I moved to the iron rear door and pulled at the knob. The bottom came free but the area around the knob remained tight. My injured hand, then, assisted my grip and I painfully yanked again.

This time, the door dragged open. Without much consideration for what laid beyond the threshold…I crossed over.

The air inside was dry and musty like an archaic mausoleum which had been sealed tightly for centuries. The only light available came from the street lamps that shone dimly through the soaped front windows silhouetting the mounds of deserted automotive inventory inside. The ground was so thick with fine dust, that it felt like sand over concrete, crunching and scratching under every footfall.

The only common vestige which lay between the contrasting realms of the indoors and outdoors were the intermittent scampers of rodent refugees, decisively more timid than their weather worn brethren.

As my eyes adjusted to the darkness, I searched for signs of Al. I called his name out twice, but received no answer.

I could feel my wounded palm begin to swell. I tried not to even consider the measure of possible infection. Nonetheless, the pain had begun to ascend up my wrist. My dauntless curiosity waned.

"Down here!" called Al's raspy voice from a lighted doorway.

I could have sworn I had, only moments ago, walked past a petrified pile of boxes where he now hung in hazed view. He appeared at the top of a flight of stairs, from which an amber glow emanated, warming the lifeless surroundings.

Al smiled a trustworthiless smile and motioned for me to follow him. Having already traveled too far to recant, I descended into the netherworld with my guide.

The stairs were splintered wooden planks, just as I had remembered them, smoothed and unevened by decades of bipedal traffic. Al's bony frame loped down the flight making virtually no sound. My own footfalls, however, were accompanied by a decisively unstealthy creak, loudly heralding my arrival.

I expected, at any moment, to catch my first glimpse of the old man, aged, eccentric and justified in his desertion of his family…his son. More likely was a pit filled to the ankles with more rodent vermin set to defend their diseased breeding cavern.

But the cellar, aside from the torches that lined the wall, was barren of any life save Al and myself.

There was more inventory however. But it bore no resemblance to anything remotely automotive. There were dusty unopened bottles of Choc-ola lined against the near concrete wall, their contents dried and rotted from within. There were rusty cases of tin canned Purple Passion and Hillbilly Juice and Cherokee Red and Cherry-Strawberry Cotton Club. And each cylinder bore the outmoded pull-tabs that once seemed born to every unweeded sidewalk and trash-laden playground. There were scores of boxes of plastic models from a forgotten era of popular fantasy: The Jupiter 2, the Mach 5, the Black Beauty, the Munstermobile, and the Phantom Cruiser. There were Pez dispensers of the Green Hornet, Yackie Doodle, the Impossibles, Motor Mouse and Auto Cat. There were rubber gorillas and tarantulas. There were old back issues of Down Beat stacked meticulously to the middle of 1970 along with Angela Davis flyers and "Mad About Mad" paperbacks. And all other liquids, hair care products, cleaners, or pest repellents, were preserved in a fraying fishnet basket of aerosol cans, like forgotten doomsday soldiers, still awaiting orders to batter the witless ozone. A giant one-speed bicycle leaned regally on its kickstand, packing enough steel in its bulk to hold its own in a head on ordeal with a semi. The walls were decorated with signs like "1/2 Gallon Ice Cream 89 Cents" and "Wise Barbecue Pig Skins 2 for 1".

The cellar was in fact, an untended shrine commemorating the days of the old man's store when business was solid and the future was certain. Conspicuous by their absence though, were…

"Drugs." muttered Al. "They here." he said as if to reassure my unspoken query.

He shuffled toward a warped wooden door and swung it open, releasing a swarm of flies, but revealing nothing pharmaceutical. Only a cracked, filthy, overflowing commode was visible. He unzipped his pants, turned back to me and smiled a Belzecuzean smile with his yellow red-rimmed eyes as his urine spattered against the piles already there.

When he finished, he zipped himself, turned, and pushed through a side wall.

"C'mon." he called as the wall closed behind him.

I held my breath and walked toward the commode. I fought my curiosity to look down as I passed the feculent pile. Unfortunately, I stole a glimpse of the tunneling colony of maggots that almost returned my most recent supper. Instinctively, I lunged through the wall entrance holding my innards.

As above, Al had adeptly disappeared. The room where I stood was lit by flickering fluorescent tubes that almost strobed normal vision. Strewn about the floor were stained cartons and shattered bottles of old pills and expired liquids.

The coated tablets and capsules formed a faded fragmented rainbow of beaded hues from red/pink to blue/azure to fusia/yellow, cracked and corroded in rivers of dried, sticky brown elixirs. Broken glass and smeared labels were adhered to virtually every cardboard or concrete surface.

Strangely, amidst the pharmaceutical carnage, the odor was sweetly stale, like the smell of a candy store surviving the stench of a dilapidated building.

Crunching pills and glass beneath my feet, I navigated through the garbage to a swinging wooden door.

This room was a chronological documentation of ethical deterioration. On a bookshelf in the far left corner sat a black, frayed, dog-eared King James positioned in utter abandonment. A fresher Koran protruded next to it, but its intact paper cover denoted equal disdain by its lack of use. Yellowed texts of *The Vision of Piers Plowman* and *The Divine Comedy* looked worn as reference material rather than literature as was Dioscorides' *Materia Medica*. Books on Palestinian persecution, Apartheid and medieval European caste societies sat more pertinently to the right. Then there was the dustless shelf of PDRs from 1950 to 1969 leaning against the *Hoffman Studies*. There were countless volumes pertaining to ancient and contemporary alchemy from India to Peru to Romania to Dahomey to the Bayou. And finally, in present use stacked on a nearby table were the speculative scribings regarding Life Beyond Life, Life after Life, Re-animation, and Soul Transference.

Next to the bookshelf was a small but cluttered laboratory area, full of test tubes, graduated cylinders, beakers and Bunsen burners surrounding a sink. Two of the burners were presently ignited.

Then there were the familiar trappings, which caused the pores of my flesh to rise.

A 19-inch black and white television perched on a three-legged wooden table, replete with chipped plastic VHF and UHF dials buzzed erratically to itself. The broken chrome-colored antenna was extended by a misshapened copper coat hanger. Next to the grainy untuned set sat a gray, dual speakered turntable which folded neatly out of its casing. The hallowed grooves of Horace Silver played soothingly between the intermittent pops of scratches and scars. A tattered vinyl black recliner was stationed four paces in front of the "entertainment center". Next to the chair was a broken end table bound precariously together with electrical tape. It supported a smoking ashtray, a half-drained 12-ounce glass and an empty bottle of Taylor.

"Old habits…" came a voice best described as my own. "…are like old friends: Comfortable, reliable and…enduring the tests of life…and death."

I whirled and was shocked by the toothy, bearded smile of the old man…alive!

For an occasion I had pursued for almost twenty years I found no words to speak upon its arrival. I simply stared into his face searching for some impostor's charade and finding none. Only the fact that he had not aged a day from the moment I saw them shut the casket beckoned pale doubt. Indeed, he appeared almost as refreshed as he had in his college photographs nearly two score to the past. His pharmacy jacket was perfectly white with an emblazoned blue RX symbol beneath his left shoulder. His creased, black trousers were without a wrinkle. And his black rubber-treaded shoes were freshly shined.

"Look at your hand." he said with no pretense of concern.

I held up the hand that had nearly numbed beyond pain, and noted the bluish green discoloration under the swelling.

"Al, get my son some Bactine, will you?" he spoke, as if to a domestic servant. "And some gauze."

I heard some rustling from a closet I had just now noticed, and in another instant Al shuffled forward carrying a dusty gray, once white, plastic bottle of Bactine and gauze. He handed me both products as if to say "I ain't no nurse" and then leaned back on the laboratory counter.

I looked at the expiration date on the bottle. "8/74" it read. I looked up at my father and he smiled encouragement. Relying on my memory of his wisdom, I flipped open the top and squeezed a runny, mustard colored substance onto my hand.

By the measure of pain searing through my arm, I immediately concluded that whatever oozed from the dirty wretched bottle was not Bactine. I suppressed a howl of pain, then shot my father an angry glance.

"Don't look at me." he said with mild annoyance, "Squeeze your hand!"

Again, trusting his expertise in such matters, I closed my aching hand as best I could.

"Harder!" he demanded.

I squeezed harder and felt the flesh in my palm tear open. I could see blood and puss running between my fingers. When I opened my hand, the swelling was gone. I took the gauze and hastily wiped away the drying blood. All that remained were three holes where the fence had poked through and a yellow stain in my palm. The pain had subsided.

"Did I sense a degree of feint-heartedness on your part?" the old man asked with a wry grin.

"That wasn't the Bactine I used to know." I replied. "I thought it wasn't supposed to hurt!"

"Anything that doesn't hurt doesn't do any good." he pronounced firmly. "Remember that...always."

He seemed all at once to dispense with frivolity with this statement, but quickly righted himself and continued.

"The Bactine you 'used to know' was a greasy placebo designed to dry the teary eyes and runny noses of scraped-kneed children with the comforting knowledge that 'mommy' had done something 'helpful'. I added an active geo-biological virus that cauterizes and disinfects. The perfect healant for those who have a high threshold for pain."

"Virus..." I muttered.

"Don't worry. It's been basement tested, basement approved." he said with only a small joke in his voice. "Besides, look at me. I've tried every thing down here at least once and while I may have lost an appetite or two, I certainly haven't lost my life."

"Or mind?" I put in.

The old man frowned mild irritation at the glancing insult. In the corner of my eye, I saw Al shift onto his feet.

"Son," he began. "I know you've got to be...wondering what I'm doing here...why I left the way I did..."

"So a smidgen of common sense has fought its way free?" I said with annoyance.

Anger flashed across the old man's face, but was quickly suppressed. Al glanced at him, surprised by his apparent restraint.

The old man nodded to me acknowledging the insult, then dropped slowly into his chair and reclined comfortably.

"I see your mother has bequeathed you her tongue's whip." he said as he lifted a fresh Kent to his lips and lit the end. "The profanity is missing, but the ilk is unmistakable. Nevertheless dear son, if anger is all you have stored up for your father after all these years, I beg you: take your leave. You were never invited!"

He leaned his head back, closed his eyes and exhaled a lengthy stream of thick smoke through his nostrils. Al turned and slunk back to the storage closet. In that moment, it was as if I had never arrived. The old man's indifference was a weapon I had come ill-prepared to combat. I could have exited this moment for another twenty years and his world, such as it was, would remain unfettered. While my world would be forever an uncompleted puzzle, the missing pieces sealed away in the recesses of the old man's basement.

With my confrontational stratagem collapsed to shambles, I stepped in front of the chair and attempted to address him in earnest.

"Certainly after all of this time, I didn't come here simply to berate you." I spoke. "But for nearly twenty years I had to live without a father. A father who I find was not dead after all, but alive and well. I have no axe to grind nor anger to vent. I just need to know…why?"

His eyelids lifted slowly, like the enormous window shades of a public library. He looked on me as if I had asked him for lint out of his pocket…as if the bother wasn't worth the effort. Then he smiled again.

"Why?" he said lazily. "You haven't seen that commercial on television? 'Why ask why?' Some things don't have clear answers. They simply are as they are and that's it. Accept it."

"I do accept those things that men have no ability to affect." I said, aggravated by his dark jocularity. "But you and you alone orchestrated this…farcical self-abduction. And for who's benefit? Not mine! Not your mother who wept over your counterfeited grave site! And certainly not your wife…my mother, who strapped the tattered remnants of our family to her back and carried your burden."

"Your mother," he said tightly, leaning forward in the recliner, "always had a better way. I never in nearly fifteen years of marriage uttered a syllable she didn't contradict. If I said something was so, then by her reckoning, it simply could not be. My 'passing' was nothing less than her long-awaited opportunity to finally 'get it right'…'have things HER way'! If in twenty years of matriarchy after my 'passing', she discovered even a shred of humility, then my influence in 'death' had much more value than my continuance as her whipping post!"

"Hmh." I responded, weighing carefully my next words. "Sounds like 'true love' sir. How wonderful."

There was a pause. Then with suddenness, he kicked down the recliner's footrest and sprung to his feet, never unlocking the grip his eyes held on my own.

"Boy…speak not of what you know not." he said in a deep growl of mammalian propriety. "I spent decades wading through the bevy of whores and heifers and mata haris and succubi that God, for no good reason other than to confound a man's sensibilities, put on this earth. To me, sex was sadistic pleasure and 'love' was just a word people used to sanitize their…our depravity. Then I met your mother: Beautiful, intelligent, strong-willed, to a fault, maybe, volatile (lord knows she was that) and true as the good earth to a thriving forest. I was unborn before I met her and my unworthiness was the only factor that justified my departure. Nothing short of selfishness could have allowed me to remain in her company. So I left!"

The old man spoke these words with sadness absent of regret. I was staggered by the tragedy of his conclusion. Yet his blood in me understood it.

He read my expression for any further questions on the matter of his husbandly affections. He found none. He, then, breathed a heavy smoke filled sigh, and returned to his chair. His eyes grew lazy again, when I broached a new line of questioning.

"So what about me?" I asked, simply.

"Hmm?" he filled, as if no such thought had ever occurred to him.

"What about me?" I repeated with emphasis. "I mean…I spent the most formative years of my life without a father…"

"Formative years?!" he cut in. "Are you married yet?"

"No sir."

"Well don't talk to me then about formative years. Get married! Trust me, *those* will be the most formative years of your life. Anything prior to that is nothing more than a testosterone induced stupor. You don't need a father for those years. What you need is a box of Trojans, a vile of penicillin and a tongue that carries a short after-taste."

From behind a half closed door, I could hear Al's echoing cackle as he affirmed the old man's conviction with a rousing hoot.

As he leaned back in his recliner I could see him measuring my countenance for a reaction. I managed to maintain some composure.

"I needed you." I continued. "There were so many things…so many…feelings I had at different junctures of my life. And I could feel the kindred part of myself that was you, reliving those same moments in my present. I felt myself understanding you more every day you were gone. But there was no one there to understand me."

"I don't follow." he claimed.

"I had questions…about me!" I continued, with desperate clarity. "Questions, only you could have answered."

"Like what." he said coldly.

The broad-ended query left me silent.

"I know," he said in preparedness to mock, "things like why you can't grow a full beard between your ears and your mouth. Or why you sometimes wake up in the middle of your sleep with a face full of warm drool. Or why you love the whine of blues but detest the twang of country. Or why you get a big hard-on every time you see a dark, skinny, little Italian girl with big tits…but never have the guts to do anything about it."

He doused the remainder of his cigarette in the ashtray. Then he leaned back again with his fingers clasped together, his head tilted slightly sideways and continued: "You often wonder how you can feel so alone in a room crowded with acquaintances, yet be perfectly consoled in the comfort of an empty house away from 'prying' eyes. I mean, you love humanity but you can't stand to be around humans! You wonder why you feel so gifted but are afraid to peek inside the wrapping. You wonder why everything and everyone around you is never good enough…including yourself! And why is it that though you hate to be cast as a leader, the mantle of leadership always lands in your lap? And why must you always, always have empathy for the party with whom you conflict? And why are you so staunch in the defense of your honor, yet so grossly unresilient in the pursuit of your dreams? And how can you be so selfish with your time, yet so careless of your fate?"

As he finished, it felt as if all the blood in my body had stopped to listen. I could not feel the floor beneath my feet nor my arms at the shoulder. I could only manage to blink away a tear that had welled in testimony to how this spectacularly unshocking spoken truth had pierced me.

He interluded the brief silence with the shake of another Kent from a pack in his front pocket. Then he flipped open a lighter, lit the end and birthed a new cloud of azure.

"Why ask why, boy." he said in a disdainfully heavy voice. "Fate preordains that we are who and what we are. We can forestall some manifestations of our characters. We can clothe and comb and smirk away the flaws for short stretches of time. We can lie about our convictions and affinities until we drown in our drivel. But innate predilection will always fight its way to the surface and govern the summation of our movements. And not all the grease-paint and costuming…and money on Earth can make it any other way. I know. I tried."

Just as his voice trailed away, a buzzer went off. Al bolted over to the lab area and hastily lifted a beaker from its perch above its burner.

"Done?" queried the old man.

"I think." answered Al frowning at the purplish-blue mixture."

"Finally." he replied with notable relief.

"So you were going to tell me what brought you here." I asked, trying to back away from the mounting malaise I had beckoned.

"Tired of comparing karmas already?"

"Yes."

"Very well. I could have returned to D.C., but what for? This…this place had been my crowning achievement. My only obstacle seemed to be that other business pursuits were determined to succeed me. There was one religious charlatan who turned my store into a 'church'! No pews, just steel chairs, probably stolen from a local grade school. No altar, just a wooden table. No organ, only an out of tune piano tinier than the one we had in our living room. But the reverend was adept at pimping the words of the Lord and his gullible parish filled the store every Sunday from the cooler to the magazine rack...or where they had once been. I, of course, resided where you see me now. But the impromptu weekday activity made my comings and goings difficult, and the stomping and carrying on Sundays less tolerable."

"So you ran them off?" I asked.

"Not exactly." he grinned in fond reflection. "You see the 'reverend', had a lustful eye for the younger calves that comprised his flock. And on many such aforementioned impromptu occasions, he would conduct private counseling sessions to young virgins on the virtue of loving only Christ, the church, and himself...his personal addendum to the Holy Trinity. Needless to say my work was frequently interrupted by the squealing and braying that accompanied the ceremonial sacrifice of cherry blossoms on the floor above or more often in the bathroom next door."

"So you called one of the girls' parents?"

"I called all of the girls' parents."

"And they had him arrested?"

"No. They killed him."

"What?"

"During the last service, he was strapped to the 'altar' and stabbed by each member of the parish. As I recall, the turnout was particularly good that day."

"The body?"

"Ground to burger and spirited off to the Red Onion's walk-in freezer by Al.

"No police?"

"Oh definitely police. But with only bloodstains to rely upon, the lazy lawmen concluded on a pagan ritual and the slaughter of some hapless animal. At least they were partly correct. Regardless, their reliable ineptitude was greatly appreciated. The 'church' was boarded up and I regained my privacy."

My stomach shifted at the matter-of-fact fashion in which the old man recounted so horrific a tale. I also concluded that whenever I departed from under the store, I would not be detouring to the Red Onion to pick up my burgers.

"So how was the auto parts store disposed of?" I asked in anticipation of another grisly story.

"Easily." he answered. "And without incident. Actually, our co-existence wasn't very troublesome. He kept regular hours and didn't use the downstairs bathroom at all. However, there was the matter of financing my work down here. So I had Al back-door his merchandise. The poor man had alarms, sonitrol, the security of Fort Knox, I think. He fired several employees, certain he was being ripped off from the inside, but he had no idea. Finally, while perusing his mail, we came upon a check for a bank loan. The poor wretch had even taken a second mortgage on his house. Well, Al forged his signature and we were set up financially. Needless to say, the owner showed up to open up one morning and the state had chained the doors. I never heard a man cry so loud. If he only knew."

"I heard his wife left `im and he kill hisself!" Al laughed.

"Hmm." pondered the old man. "Maybe that does qualify as an incident."

"And you could care less that you ruined his life?" I asked in dismay.

"Dog eat dog, boy." he said in an even growl. "When famine hits the African plain and the antelope population starves and rots away, the carnivores who once hunted side by side and often shared their kill, feast upon each other. So it is in a man's world. In my youth, I was a fool. When I had nothing, I had little desire to plunder the selfish ones who had something. And when I had something, I hoped that others might be moved by my magnanimity. But alas, what I couldn't give was stolen. And on the day that I handed over the keys to my life's work, this store, the carnivores laughed at what an easy mark I had been. So I say: Dog eat dog. Or…`man eat man'."

The old man frowned for a moment as if retracing the pain of that one regretful loss. Then he rose quickly from the chair as if to sever himself from the memory.

"Well son," he said with a short sigh, "you haven't asked me the one thing I was certain you would."

"And that is…"

"How."

"How?"

"Yes. How I managed to die three days past Christmas and wind up here.

"I guess, finding that you lived at all made the `how' less important." I realized.

"Well let me tell you something: Drugs can be amazing when put to their proper use. Back then, and even now, everyone is looking for a good excursion. Do you know what the ultimate excursion is? It's when you fall asleep in front of the television and wake up in the sterile stock room of a funeral parlor three days later. You see, I hadn't planned to leave…or not just yet anyway. But one evening this half-ass Creole who claimed to have grown up on the bayou came into the center where I worked. He said he needed some Mysoline to fight back the tremors from his habit, but had no means by which to pay for it. So he offered me this dark yellow powder that he claimed 'made the dead walk down home'. Not really believing him, but wanting very badly to get his effluvium out of my office I made the transaction. That night I tasted it on the tip of my finger, and it burned like cajun spice. I tasted a little more, enough to give me some kind of affect but nothing happened. I waited a few hours and concluded I'd been taken in. So I dumped the rest on a pile of pork rinds and started drinking. In my time I'd experimented with valium, prolixin, moban and a few other tranquilizers, but nothing had ever dropped me like this. I dreamt about an autopsy, an embalming, the rings of Dante's inferno, and a world in which I never lived. When I awoke, I was dressed to be buried and Al was looking down at me in my coffin."

"You're not serious." I said in disbelief. "How do you survive an autopsy and an embalming?"

"Chemicals." he said with a smile. "If nothing else, God almighty is the greatest chemist in the universe."

"So you're a zombie." I over simplified.

"I'm what the barefoot bongo beaters mistake for a zombie." he said with a frown. "I'm more of a xenogenetic mutation."

"Mutation?" I asked with puzzlement. "But you're fine, right?"

"Not really." he replied in a foreboding tone.

Without warning, he walked over to his makeshift laboratory and picked up a scalpel. He slowly cut a triangular incision along the inside of his jawbone above his neck. I thought certainly amidst these bizarre circumstances he had chosen this odd moment to cut his own throat in front of my very eyes.

But instead, a purplish-black puss spilled out onto the collar and chest of his pharmacy jacket. And I knew it wasn't blood. He peeled up the flesh from behind his ears and revealed the features beneath. His hands were covered with the thick mucousy discolorant as he worked to tear the false flesh from his eye sockets and nose. As he worked back to his scalp the sickening ripping sound of severing hair strands was nauseating.

When he was finished, before me stood a moist bluish pink skulled desecration of the human form. And amazingly, I could still recognize him through the garish disfigurements.

"I learned the hard way son." he said in the familiar voice. "If you fuck around with God's creation long enough, you'll get your DNA validation canceled!"

He chuckled more to himself than at Al or me.

"How…how long…" I stammered, trying to collect my composure.

"Like this?" he smiled a lipless grin. "After about two years, I thought I had it made…then things began to shrivel and…drop off. It didn't hurt particularly much, but my appearance became rather ghastly. After a couple of years in scarves and hats, I found a way to regenerate the skin. Unfortunately, my new hemoglobin would suck away the moisture and in a few weeks…Halloween again. I tried to experiment with growth hormones but that failed miserably. Did wonders for the rats, though, wouldn't you say?"

Al laughed again.

The old man savagely swung about and pummeled Al with his fists and forearms. Never had I seen the old man vent himself with violent rage so unchecked. Al curled up like a cringing submissive cur under the profusion of strikes, his bony knees covering the majority of his face. Still, when the barrage was concluded, Al's lip was split open and a large swelling quickly formed at the center of his brow. There was never once, any resistance.

"Cackling mongrel child!" the old man spat between tightly clenched teeth. "How could I have ever thought you'd amount to more than a festering canker on the face of humanity?"

"Yes, sir." said Al, sheepishly ignorant of the old man's insult.

"Yes sir?" persisted the old man. "You don't even understand what I just said do you?"

Al rolled his yellowed eyes away in shame.

"Do you?" the old man shouted, kicking Al's knees from his face.

"No sir." Al responded.

"A little louder!" demanded the old man. "You can howl like a boar with his testicles in a bear trap when you `think' something is funny. But as soon as the air thickens with a molecule of substance, you tumble into an autistic fog."

"No sir!" said Al belatedly.

"Is that a dispute?" teased the old man.

"No sir." answered Al, resolved to dejection.

The old man turned his hideous visage back upon me and smiled as I watched the tendons and veins lift the sides of his mouth.

"If I had only seen then, what I see now." the old man spoke, with mild regret. "Al, here, was my first project: The handwriting on the wall. The first time I saw him, he was stealing Pez off the candy counter. Instead of turning him over to the police, I lectured him and gave him a job. That's what I would have wanted someone to do for me when I was in his shoes! So what did Al do to express his gratitude? He stole from me again! And when I splintered a broom handle on his empty skull, he whimpered like a misbegotten hound. But never once contemplated the error of his ways."

Al stared blankly into space holding his head as if determined to stem the tirade.

"Still, unlike his own wayfaring addict parents, I refused to give up on him. Like some angel, inebriated with duty, I was determined to rescue him from his cretinus lineage. Over the past twenty years, while fighting for my very existence, I paid thousands of dollars in bail money, abortion fees, penicillin injections, drug rehabs, cocaine offspring, strawberry girlfriends and any other insult to the human race his squalid existence could muster!"

The old man knelt down to where Al sat and snatched him by his thinning, unkempt hair. Al cringed at the closeness of the old man's hideous visage...a sight to which he had never become accustomed.

"Now you're almost forty and what have you made of yourself: A homeless 'step and fetch it' for a dead pharmacist! The very air in your lungs would better serve some bacterial growth on the underside of a dead animal's carcass than sustain your life. But here you sit. There must be a reason."

"Who are we to say?" I asked.

"Who?" the old man said rising to his feet. "I'll tell you who. The man who went searching into the fathomless cesspool of despair in the hopes of finding one ash of redemption among the thousands of 'Als' in this city...only to find that they cared more for my failure than for their own...salvation. I'm to say, dear son.

"But fear not." he said walking over to the cooled solution on the laboratory table. He lifted up a concocted y-shaped plastic apparatus with two syringes on the end of the dual prongs. He filled the single end with the purplish blue solution. Then he stabbed one of the syringes into his arm without the slightest wince. The clear prong in his arm drew a thick dark brown liquid which represented what his blood had become. The two substances merged at the second syringe and chemically transformed to a brilliant bright scarlet.

"I don't look this way because my flesh is teeming with life." said the old man with dark sincerity. "I am dying."

Strangely, in lieu of what I'd seen, these words came almost as a relief. For years I had been teased with the question of his life or death. Tonight, under the store, I would have my answer. And it didn't matter which!

"This body of mine is done." he continued. "But it doesn't have to be the end. Both of you, are like flip sides of the same coin. And in my eyes you both represent the future...as it should be."

He turned and offered Al an insincere gaze of fondness. There was fear in Al's eyes, but he knew the old man had never done him a wrong turn. He stood and walked, childlike to the old man's side…almost apologetically for falling short in his master's eyes.

The old man let the second syringe dangle and looked at me. "This solution will allow my essence to continue through the recipient. I've been able to combine the old Indian ritual of transferring the soul to alternate animate life forms with the Turkish root that reconfigures brain patterns. Tonight, we'll all become a little part of one another. Al?"

Al closed his eyes and offered his forearm as tiny beads of sweat rolled down his temples. To the old man something enormous was about to occur. To Al, it was little more than a new type of fix.

The old man never touched the second syringe. He reached behind the burners and pulled out a third syringe with a six inch needle. He winked at me and then violently stabbed Al in the side of the neck.

Al's yellow eyes seem to blaze white for the first time as they burst open. He turned to attack, but the blood spurting profusely from his throat became a larger priority. He tried to pull the needle out straight but his panic caused him to break it off instead. Dark red lesions formed on the surfaces of his skin as he struggled in futility to curtail the fatal spillage. Finally, Al who had been unable to make a sound, loosed a series of piercing anguished death screams. The last saw his tongue fly from his bloodied mouth and scamper across the room as if it had mutated a life of its own.

"In the orient, it pays to check your prescription." the old man said with an evil grin. He kicked the body and it cracked like a thin clay shell.

I was frozen with horror.

"You see son," he said in an overly calm voice, "People like him rot our society from the inside out. Like the ancient lepers, they're pleas are pitiable but their touch is deadly. The only thing they find more disgusting than your good fortune is the prospect of they're own hard work to attain the same.

"When the bubonic plague marauded its way through Europe in the fourteenth century, there was no measure too extreme to eradicate its deadly influence. Blankets, buildings and people were burned in no small measure to stop its spread. I submit to you now, that no small measure can be taken to eradicate the pestilence that eats away at our world! There are so many good people out there being infected every day. And we say 'help and understand' those who would rather see us dead. I say let's herald the rescue of civilization by ridding us of the Als among us!"

He held up the needle for me as he had for Al before.

"Join me, son. You have the strength and the vitality. I have the knowledge. Together, we can…do a lot of good."

As before, a part of me understood full well the inertia behind his reasoning: His love of the 'Als' in conflict with having been betrayed by the 'Als'. I understood his anger, his frustration and his lust for revenge. Yet, at the time, some part of me thought he was wrong.

Then suddenly, the room was plunged into darkness. I ran toward where I thought the exit was and tripped over the fragmented carrion. Quickly, I regained my feet but felt the sharp pain of the needle enter my shoulder and lost consciousness.

As I stated at the beginning, I have no idea how long I'd been unconscious until moments ago. But when morning came, I found that everything had turned out well.

I picked up a grease stained bag and finished the last two french fries rolling around in the salt at the bottom.

I checked my bank book having totally forgotten its balance and decided that rather than go to work, I would stop off at the drug store for some Kents, and then visit a pharmaceutical warehouse nearby.

After all, time was of the essence, since the past, present and future had become one and the same…on a frozen December evening under the store.

finis

LOST MERCEDES

Along my sacred journey down the narrow path I came to a divide not clearly marked. That is to say, the divide was not unmarked, but the markings themselves denoting the route best chosen were astutely unclear to me.

Oh, there were lurid hints as to what wondrous sights and sounds did or did not await my fancies dependent upon which road I chose to take. The straight path promised little or no amusements upon which my intellect could be satiated. The destiny was certain. The outcome was assured. And I would be none the poorer, none the wiser and none the troubled along the unfretted trail leading toward my ordained destiny.

But from the curved path I heard music and song which, absent of a finely tuned ear, could have been taken for the joyful noises of our coveted scripture. I saw bright lights beckoning my plagued secular curiosity. And of course, cousin Nick stood closely to my ear purporting, and I quote: "the splendiferous company of feminine pulchritude no mortal male of sound mind should intention himself to dismiss."

Now mind you, I have always considered myself wise enough to filter cleanly cousin Nick's pontifications which mirage reprobacy under the veil of inert neutrality. In fact, as one of a singular mind and a certainty in faith, I had always taken great pleasure in the recognitions of false trappings and permeable wrappings with unpliable resolve. For man is always put to the test. And such being the case, I had taken good consolation from the routine of my always passing rather well.

I considered the depth of the worst possible resolution that could manifest itself along the crooked road. It was known for a fact that a patron from the north (like myself) had been abruptly murdered outside the same exhibitionist hall which cousin Nick now urged me to enter therein. Yet I recall that this aforementioned patron committed the most grievous error of becoming boisterously entangled with the interest of a crooked native resulting in that patron's inevitable fatality. In this demise I observed little comparative for my station since I, a spartan model of unemotional stoicism, would ne'er victim myself by such doltish entanglements. Nor did I believe it plausible that the surety of my soul could be ruptured by females clearly set aside for no more than profligate recreation.

Therefore, as I descended along the alternate route I reveled proudly in my certainty. For I had frequented similar such halls filled to a mortal man's avarice with beauteous naked shells of lavishly, though scantily, adorned temptresses and ne'er once exited with little more than a lightened billfold and the faded recollections of physically endowed, spiritually desolate, libidinous trollops. Thus, as I passed through the golden plated gate of cousin Nick's depraved abode, everything appeared in the order in which I had anticipated.

At the entrance, thickly muscled sentries swaggered about, grimly inspecting the patrons as they paid out exorbitant tolls to pass into the dimly lit, loudly serenaded exhibition hall. The seating arrangements featured stage chairs for those intent on the indulgence of precise scrutiny and open ended expenditures. The gallery tables suited those, like myself, contented to view proceedings from a distance wringing a designated sum of funds for their optimum time and value. Though not surprisingly, the relevance of time quickly diminished upon my order of the first predictably ice diluted stein of spirits.

As I nestled into my seat, cousin Nick contentedly abandoned me to my own dalliance as I sat, witlessly, not amongst the crowd as I perceived, but among the players on a side stage born of his clandestine designs, yet animated by ignitions of my own undoing.

I passively evaluated the bevy of entertainers as they seductively revealed their personal virtues to the gratuitous suitors who compensated them for their "amorous" expositions. Ranking the largest, smallest, tallest, thinnest, youngest, eldest, wildest, sweetest, saddest amongst the sad was a frivolous pastime I best enjoyed in such a desperately iniquitous setting.

For a time, my attentions were fixed upon a tall, slender woman I fancied a university student by her youth and upper-middle strata collegiate aloofness, who by my reckoning, had foolishly concluded that it was best for her to be recompensed for what she had once peddled freely in dormitory bedrooms and fraternity house attics, than to profitlessly remain mired in her indiscriminate campus whoredom.

And of course, there was the obligatory bleach maned mannequin who had seen as much of the surgeon's scalpel as most see of a bread knife amongst their dining utensils. She smiled, galloped, and brayed about her stage like a badly doped mare, flaunting her debased humanity as lecherous suitors cheered her to greater depths of humiliation. Indeed, an overzealous patron was goaded by her ungenuine behests to encroach upon the physical barriers of "propriety". This, in turn, roused the thickly muscled sentries to violently immobilize him and dispatch his expensively accoutered, quickly unconscious frame out of the rear exit with little care and horrid expedience.

But while the severely undone gentleman's forcibly induced departure made splendid fare for levitous exchanges between myself and others around me, none were so riotous in their genuine expressions as the poor old emaciated Asian man who best resembled an underpaid custodian who had recently been bestowed his meager monthly wage. While the matter of his tastes were beyond reproach, as he monopolized through heavy dolings the attentions of a royally attractive, buxomly blessed brunette, the manner in which he pathetically importuned her leased affections through the clutching of her hands and his crudely butchered dialect became the inane target of our cruel hilarity. The indentured woman sat attentively in his company for some time, wrestling dizzily to make sense of his verbal groping and frantic gesticulations. Finally, a manager came to thankfully translate their transaction and the satisfied customer and his sublet escort were led up the stairs to consummate their private discussion.

At this moment I found myself cheerfully indebted to the fulfilled promises of cousin Nick and his hall of misguided morality. For though I stake no virtue in this fault of mine, I have always enjoyed the morose ironies surrounding the undoings of the chronically suicidal, numbering myself not among them. As it was, I found the evening to be one of unencumbered, richly satisfying leisure.

Then, a light tug on my left trouser pocket encroached upon the sanctity of my veiled sequestration.

I spun left, urgently accounting for the presence of my billfold. The billfold remained lodged yet I noted no prospect for the gesture. I quickly turned right and was immediately warmed by the vision of a smiling golden nymph with dark shortened hair neatly framed about her heaven tendered features. She obligatorily wore little in conformity to her stipendiary duties. But of what there was, I recount it as bright white and complimentary to her slight but flawless figure. Her warm smile was as luminescent as her smoothed complexion which was not at all as seductive as it was, simply charming. And as I foolishly allowed her clear emerald eyes to bore sharply into my poorly defensed sensibilities, I instinctively, with gentlemanly tact, paid complement to her favorable appearance with all the courtesy commendable to a young debutante attending her first society ball. Interestingly, upon the hearing of this, she smiled oddly as if a more crudely smithed remark should have sufficed. But even now, I say that to this lady I could have made no such comment that would have besmirched her endearing loveliness as I chose to envision her that perplexing eve.

She daintily waved her departure. And all I could invoke was a smile as my eyes guided her ascent upon a rear staircase to an upper level where she awaited her shift to officially begin. During this time she intermittently conversed with fellow performers but would now and again glance over the balustrade to prospect the scenery below.

It was during this interlude that I knowingly, ill-advisedly, mated my attentions to her every movement. The parade of immaculately sculpted, feminine perfections continued upon the stages below. And the performers often fell to even excursioning amongst the roiling, licentious crowd itself. Everyone was, in fact, particularly astounded upon the moment when the towering dominatrix who had disdainfully stalked through the hordes of patrons as if concerned with some weighty matter superseding the lustful desires of the men around her, finally unveiled her wealthy overendowments. The hall erupted with the fervored fanatical enthusiasm of an enraptured throng in attendance of a sporting event which had taken some climactic turn in favor of the home club. I did not completely ignore this event, as she admittedly bore extraordinarily mountainous protrusions of flesh. But soon after the initial wave of exaltation settled into the relentlessly pounding music, my spelled gaze wandered back to the upper pedestal, where perched my adored fixation.

I was never certain how often she looked down to observe how surely I had obsessed my longings to her favor. But it was clearly sufficient enough as proved by the turbid events which ensued.

For a short interlude, all of the performers gathered their scant belongings and disappeared out of varied exits. In another moment, along the upper walkway, each performer sequentially reappeared, marching as if in preparation for a lascivious blitzkrieg on the senses of the currency carrying voyeurs who lustfully awaited their return. In choreographed unison three lines formed at the top of three brightly lit staircases. The crowd below surged into a decadently approving murmur as the women garishly descended their alluring forms back into the dimly illuminated pits.

One line formed center stage and two bordered themselves along the walls. It was then that I heard cousin Nick's voice beckon us all to choose the one which would suit our personal pleasures.

"Choose", his mischievous voice echoed loudly within the corridors of my vacillating cerebrum. It was as if I could have had any of the score and one half displayed before the crowd upon my command of it. The very notion was odd to me in that I am not totally ashamed to confess that in no time of my life have I ever had my choice of female company, paid for or otherwise. And that even in such instances when all variables would seem to stand rigged to my favor, some utterly expected divergence would conveniently intercede to rescue the woman from my doting graces, leaving me cynical and embittered on the matter of having felt anything at all.

Of course this night should have been kilometers removed from any such thoughts. After all, by my own reckoning, I sat no more than two circles north of cousin Nick's depraved brothels wherein harlots of no virtue bartered their corrupted flesh for thin, ephemeral profits. That so near such iniquitous pandering, I could even begin to reflect upon the true merit of my tangible relationships, past and future, clearly cast my sound reasoning amongst the impaired. For Cousin Nick had certainly not invited me to the viewing of his hedonists' delights solely for the cathartic purpose of allowing me to sort through some unsolvable personal dilemma. Yet, acknowledging the foolhardiness of pursuing matters thusly, this eroded line of thought was exactly the route upon which I chose to continue.

As the performers sold off their persons to the bidding masses who proudly flagged the capricious power of their currency, I settled upon the economical decision that it would be best if I reserved my bits for sustenance alone and should merely observe from a safe distance the purchased exhibits of the other patrons. But curiosity forced me to scour the lines to see who would call forth the artless ingénue, who had smitten my affections with casually little effort.

I panned, I thought with secreted discretion, across the twisting, turning, high-heeled shapes merely to observe what would become of her. However, as I found her, still unchosen, she looked fondly upon me and expectantly held my gaze for more than passing seconds. Absent of any resolve upon which to call, I resignedly motioned her hither.

Moving cautiously, as a yearling doe through its first winter's frost, she alighted from her perch and maneuvered carefully to engage my modest company.

To my regret, she remained as exquisite in form as I had first observed her to be. She bore an elegance and an engaging genuineness that betrayed the hollowed qualifications required of her employ. We spoke briefly about what I cannot recall. My recollections held only her enchanting presence and the alias by which she named herself: Mercedes.

She gracefully unhooked her laced halter and draped it softly across my shoulder, promising my dignity no derision as I inspected her.

The sweet scent of her bright golden flesh tickled, teased and exhumed my adolescent dreams of a truest love. Her neck was long and delicately extended from her small naked shoulders. And it was gratifying to observe that her bosom bore none of the surgical scars that most of her cosmetically immodest peers had optioned to bear. Perhaps this was why other patrons had forsaken her naturalness in favor of the unnaturally gifted sirens which made manifest, their shallowed fantasies. Perhaps this was why I could hear cousin Nick cackling when it became more than apparent that I had fallen into obsession with Mercedes by the realities I had failed to refuge in my heart.

She slowly removed her other garment, yet I scarcely made notice. For her princessed presence had mesmerized me beyond the considerations of mere sensuality and desire. By her beauty and her courtesy and her singular attentions toward me I in earnest, became deludingly saddened that I had found her as I did.

Would that I could have met this seemingly cheerful young woman in a clothing shoppe assisting customers with their sizing. Or in a tavern serving food or drink rather than the gifts God had so graciously bestowed upon her. Or in a park sharing the wonder of young ducklings embarking upon their inaugural plunge. Or in the corner of a library cleaving through the labyrinth of some weighty subject wherein I had once expertly delved. Or on the roadside in need of hasty assistance to meet some important engagement. Or through friends or relatives who always took upon themselves the need to induce such meetings on my behalf.

Would that I could have laid eyes on this cherished bloom of feminine splendor in the swirling fields of God's grace, rather than in cousin Nick's ranked dungeon of squalid morality. Herein, my judgment had no light that it could follow. I could only scramble to rely poorly on the irrationality of my mortal instincts.

As she carefully replaced her clothing, I generously recompensed her for her attentions. She smiled graciously and then, to my deepest chagrin, quickly disappeared.

In her absence I attempted to reinitiate my merry mood. I tried painfully to smear my fond memory of her into the indistinguishable homogeneity of her libertine peers. But some force, unseen, held her out from the others. It may well have been the squelched cries of some suppressed desperation. But the fine weave of its tapestry, in retrospect, bore the ilk of something else rather sinister.

A third of an hour passed while I absorbed the vulgar dances of the sculpted succubi who stalked the glowing stages, collecting bounties for the lewdness of their talents. Disinterest slowly ebbed my enthusiasm as did the costliness of heavily diluted sustenance.

I found myself growing gradually annoyed by the monotony of cousin Nick's hall of spiritual desolation. But suddenly, as remarkably as she had vanished, beauteous Mercedes rematerialized at my shoulder as if cued by the very flow of my thoughts for her.

She simply stood looking out over the cauldron of libidinous nudity as if reflecting upon some greater question of humanity's profound existence. At that moment, fully clothed, she appeared more than simply beautiful, but pensively, angelically wondrous…configured by my own illusions of female perfection. With no further consideration for our deplorable surroundings or the regretful circumstances by which we met, I endeavored to engage her personal convictions.

I was careful at first, offering her monies for her mere proximity. But when this seemed to matter little, I pursued the avenue of a natural discourse.

The first question that leapt from my tongue was to query as to why she, clearly bred at some point to the elegance she bore effortlessly, had fallen to so unseemly a mode of earning her daily bread.

She smiled plainly, though sufficient enough to sway me to the favor of her response, even before the hearing of it. She explained simply that the remuneration for her performances was the only means by which she could sustain the life-style which made her most comfortable. By her recount, at some past interval, though in this she was oddly vague, she had entertained other opportunities which did not suit her.

I then inquired as to the perceptions her loved ones harbored toward her dubious occupation. And though the least of my intentions was to, in any way, affect injury upon her fairest person, it was made manifest through her poorly divertive countenance that I had massaged upon a sensitive wound.

Nonetheless, she optioned to smile cheerfully again, offering that her family cared little, and her acquainted beau cared enough.

My response, (and even now, I cannot confirm its point of origin), was that were I her acquainted beau, I could not allow anyone for whom I cared so deeply, to continue for another moment debasing that which God hath so amply and abundantly gifted upon her.

She suddenly looked upon me with the defenseless eyes of a confused child. I attempted feebly to withdraw from my words with a limply fashioned, divertive smile of my own. But she locked my unsecured countenance with a pained expression, either saddened or angered that I had dared to circumvent the law of cousin Nick's hedonistic hall by the inference of emotional attachment.

For an instant, it was as if she stood from behind a barbed wire barricade, hopeful and faithful that some man, like myself, would prevail upon the sharpened spikes and the cabled vines to whisk her safely to the other side. Somewhere cleansed of man's incestuous decadence. Somewhere safe from the falsehoods of false favors. Somewhere where requited, unconditional love would envelop her for as long as she drew breath on God's earth. I prayed, somewhere with me.

I leaned forward and slipped my final note along the inside of her laced garter, and held it there caressing the alluring smoothness of her gentle skin. She reached up with a satin laced glove and touched my cheek suspending my awareness of space indeterminately.

With no further exchange between us, she turned and fended her way back through the careless hordes and returned to the side stage from which I had beckoned her. She mechanically removed her clothing in command to the devilish rhythms of cousin Nick's suggestive harmonies. She found my eyes once more and ingenuously smiled the irony of our ill-fated juxtaposition from across the hall.

I sat transfixed upon the vulnerable isolation of her diminutive figure, imagining myself hacking valiantly with a broad sword through the lecherous desolates which sustained her livelihood and the eroded, corrupted manacles which enslaved the virtue of her pristine soul.

At the end of the song, she once again gathered up her belongings and disappeared through a dimly lit exit.

Upon her departure, I sadly concluded that it was not within me to facilitate Mercedes' daunted liberation.

As I exited the hall and started up the crooked road toward the narrow path, my mind remained awhirl with the tautological questions surrounding my genuine feelings for beautiful Mercedes and consideration of hers for me. I even played upon the notion that if I would not rescue Mercedes to the world I most coveted, might I nurture solace in resignation to hers?

Conclusively, in the distance, from the doorway of cousin Nick's hall of misguidance and deception, I could hear him loudly hooting at the folly of my confusion. For though I wrestled with the tragedy of the lovely Mercedes' loss, he grinned his assurance that in the pit of his black kingdom, he would forever command my lost Mercedes…and hold dominion over all of her ilk.

finis

THE WISDOM OF AGNOSTIC MISOGYNY

I got laid last Friday. It was great. Without God, the world is Heaven on Earth! No guilt. No regrets. No recrimination. Just a really good time!

It was the culmination of nine days of playing slut-chess with this silly little bimbette I'd met in the library. The only reason I was there in the first place was because I was looking for a friend who was going to loan me some money. He said he'd be on the third floor but I forgot and started looking for him on the second. I had no idea where I was when I ran across this hot little library strumpet. You know: your stereotypical pint-sized, 5-foot nothing, stringy-haired whore-de-jour wearing hip-hugger jeans, a short clingy sweater to show off a stripe of bare tummy under her bra-less little boobs, and these big round glasses sitting on her nose to make her look like an intellectually reticent, slightly above-it-all, "hip chick". It was a neat costume for someone so clearly mired in the mainstream of homogeneity. But she was basically cute. And best of all, I could tell by the slight, insecure dip of her neck, that her fragile female esteem was just a tad malnourished. I could already feel my fangs sinking into her begging little throat.

We simultaneously busted each other checking each other out. Then she ducked back into her studious role, pretending to pick through some books I'd already watched her pick through. I could tell her mind went blank the moment she saw me, but she tried to play it cool. As she hung her head, and hid her eyes behind a blonde curtain of hair swinging from her head, I walked up close behind her and didn't say a word. I acted as if I were passively interested in the same stuff she was interested in, peering over her shoulder at some books and magazines dealing with the fall of Communism in eastern Europe. I got close enough to breathe on those invisible hairs on the back of her scrawny little neck, take in the whiff of a timid scent of perfume, then just snorted nonchalantly with a half-snicker and walked away.

I looked back and busted her watching me again. She did the nervous hair-flip thing, pushed her hair behind her ear and pretended to go back to what she was doing. So then I disappeared behind a row of shelves and watched her through the cracks. All of a sudden, she wasn't interested in any books or magazines. She wanted to be cool, but she was very discreetly searching around the room, trying to figure out where I went. What a feeling. I knew right then and there, I was going to fuck this girl I hadn't even met yet. It was just a matter of when.

She took a short stroll around the reading room, inspecting the endcaps, intently pretending to search for more books. But I knew full well what she was looking for. She almost found me too. But I slipped around another row of shelves just as she slowly walked by with her chin up in the air feigning every bit the diligent and focused history devotee.

Finally, she gave a heavy sigh that no one noticed but me. She returned to the table where her pile of books and magazines sat, gathered them up along with her backpack, and purposefully stalked up to the checkout counter. She moved with a subtle, huffy annoyance, as if her evening had just been crashed and burned. I figured this was the perfect time to make my move.

I quietly approached the counter and stood directly behind her again. Then, as the scraggly old librarian looked up, I raised a finger from behind my quarry's head and spoke one key word:

"Chow-ches-skew" I pronounced the name, having no clue how it was spelled. "I'm looking for a biography on Ceausescu."

The withered old librarian with the stretch marks around her wrinkled lips had no time to respond (nor did I want her to). My little library urchin spun about on cue and with a twinkle in her eye, proceeded to regurgitate every date and fact she could muster on the deposed and executed ruler of Cold War Communist Romania. All I really knew about Ceausescu was that the news had shown some really cool footage of he and his wife laying contorted on the ground after they'd been polished off by a pro-Democracy firing squad. That, and I recalled some drunken political ramblings on the subject by the lead singer of this bar-band I went to see a few weeks afterward. Otherwise, I didn't really have a clue about Ceausescu. But the neat thing was, I didn't need a clue.

Elizabeth (or "Liz" as she insisted upon being called after our first tall espresso) did all of my work for me. All I had to say was that I was working on a "paper" (which could have been paper to wipe my ass for all she knew), and she was more than willing to take over the conversation from there. I merely sipped, nodded and flashed enough "meaningful" eye contact to make her increasingly anxious.

At first, I began concocting how I would maneuver this hungry little rabbit into my snare (and onto her back). I considered a simple string of level II BS lies which usually worked in these situations. But frankly, I found that she was actually more full of shit than I was. That is, she was totally sincere about herself. But when it came to me, there wasn't anything that came out of my mouth she couldn't find some tortured excuse to agree with. The game suddenly changed and she wasn't even good at it. So instead of trying to impress her, I toyed with her post adolescent desperation by finding ways to unimpress her. It was a shameless riot. Nothing seemed to work.

I told her I was pro-homo, but anti-abortion. I told her I was raised Catholic, but hated the Pope's guts. I told her some black people are okay, but most of them bug the shit out of me. (I even referenced a fictitious genetic study to assert their intellectual inferiority, to which she vacantly responded "wow"). I told her two shots of vodka every morning helped me concentrate at work. I told her women are just as smart as men, but only the fat ugly ones don't secretly plan to get married, dump their careers and stay home with their kids. I even told her I wasn't above smacking a chick if I got really pissed off. For over an hour, I continued to pull this stinking mountain of crap out of my rear end. And she managed, somehow, to seamlessly nod and agree, shoveling up all my shit and finding ways to spread it around for fertilizer. This poor girl manufactured kismet faster than a trashy romance writer. Oh yeah. She definitely wanted it.

To make doubly sure, I even told her some really filthy jokes I wouldn't have told to a bar full of hookers and convicts. But this sheltered suburban twit didn't even blink, flashing her perky prep-school smile and acting as if I had dispensed the bawdy wit of Shakespeare during some literary seminar.

"You are sooo funny!" she grinned her expensive, pearly white dental work. Being told by a girl like this that "you are sooo funny" after a series of dirty jokes is code for "fuck me like a trailer-park skank" in educated suburbanese.

So then I decided to dictate terms. I tossed out the notion that I believed I could always tell when a relationship was going somewhere (wherever "somewhere" is) because we'd have sex on the second date. You know, most people say the third date. But I said it was a cliché (and of course, she agreed). So I told her sex on the second date was emblematic of an irresistible attraction, to which she responded with a horny nervous smile, an adjustment to her glasses and several insecure little flips and tucks of the hair again. It was so hard not to laugh in her face.

Anyway, she thanked me for the "deep" conversation and said she lived nearby so, (duh), I offered to walk her home. We hit this really dark patch of sidewalk covered by trees along this row of old brownstone apartments. She was rambling about some ex-boyfriend who'd hurt her feelings when I grabbed her, pushed her up against this huge tree, really hard, and started mashing and mauling her like something low and cheap. Her glasses and backpack disappeared just like "that". I guess she'd been rehearsing the scene in her own mind and had her moves all plotted. This was so sad. I made it rougher than normal, but she just didn't seem to care. That little tongue. That little mouth. It tasted like cherry candy. Too much cherry candy, actually. Her saliva was like cherry syrup! (What are women thinking?). Anyway, I got my hands under the sweater and the hard little boobs were kind of a disappointment. I'd been looking forward to those little knobs through three espressos. And suddenly they were a disappointment. So I went for the button on the jeans and just then, she found her coy "morality".

"Not…here" she panted and grabbed my fingers. I had to admit, for a girl offering virtually no resistance all night, she suddenly had an excellent grip. She meant it. Not here. Not tonight.

I backed up and gathered myself, acting like I felt like a jerk. That worked nicely. The cherry tongue was back in my mouth before I could lie and say I was sorry. From there, I played the rest of the night like Beaver Cleaver just to give her enough leeway to pretend I was half a gentleman. Her glasses miraculously reappeared on her face and I dug her backpack out of the bushes where she had flung it. We held hands the rest of the way to her place. I flirted like I was dying to come up to her apartment "like a typical guy" so she could turn me down like the "lady" she wasn't. She slipped me one more sliver of cherry and that was it. Her *faux honneur* had been preserved.

No, I did not call her. Calling her would have led to games. And getting tangled up in games with girls like Liz creates serial killers. Besides, the next time I saw her I wanted a gusher, not a squirt. I wanted that malnourished esteem to eat away every morsel of pride she could comprehend. I didn't want to deal with some convoluted "modern babe" confidence I'd have to sift through for a month. I didn't want a date. I wanted a human sacrifice.

Six days passed including a "dreaded" weekend before *she* called *me*. This poor little intellectual historian could only muster "what's up?" when I answered the phone. During the early part of the conversation, I decided to inject a few pregnant pauses interspersed with a yawn or two. Her response was to keep saying "so, what's up?" as if she were punching the "refresh" icon on her computer, hoping the horny exciting guy from the other night would pop up at any moment. The tension (hers, not mine) finally forced her to ask why I hadn't called over the weekend. This was too easy.

"I was busy." I answered dryly.

Women fucking hate that. "Busy". As in too busy for them. Not too busy to sit in front of the TV and watch eighteen hours of sports. Not too busy to go out and pound beers with your friends, staring at other women's asses until 3am. Not too busy to go CD shopping or give the dog a nice neat pedicure. Just too busy to call the girl who gave you her cherry tongue and let you paw her little boobs before you told her your whole name. Nothing scares a woman more than feeling irrelevant. Not rape. Not murder. At least rape or murder puts them at the center of a crime. But irrelevance? There is no greater pain.

She quizzed me about my weekend to the point where I should have been annoyed. But it was just too funny. The more she asked, the more vague I was. The less I said, the more certain she was that I had fucked somebody. In her own mind she began to fabricate a losing competition with a non-existent rival. She tried to be subtle about it, but again, she was so obvious. I actually started to feel like I was bashing a blind baby seal. The "gusher" was there for the taking. All I had to do was pick the time.

"So when are we getting together?" I finally droned monotonously.

The excitement in her voice, which she couldn't contain, was pathetic. Suddenly, she was talking in another octave. I pictured her squat-legged on her bed, bouncing her history books onto the floor with pitiable girlish glee. But then, why not? This would be the "second date". And we all "know" that if things go "well" on the second date, then it means "something".

She pretended for half a milli-second that she might be busy, loudly flipping pages in what I was to presume was her day planner. So I yawned again. Immediately, Friday night became absolutely wide open ("wide open" being the operative theme of the evening).

She asked me what I wanted to do. And I told her there was this new Drew Barrymore movie I wanted to see. Of course, I hate fucking nasty, skanky, drugged out, Drew Barrymore and her movies always suck beyond mortal endurance. But I knew it would be just the kind of vacuous romance "date" movie that would really get Liz's motor running.

"I love Drew Barrymore!" Liz shrieked, nearly popping my eardrum. "And it's got Freddie Prinze Jr. in it too!"

I thought: How does the world create such a steady stream of predictably unimaginative human beings. All this intellectual capacity people are supposed to have, flatlined into a few generic funnels of bland social conformity. If God really existed, girls like Liz wouldn't. But then, I remembered the fact that I hadn't had sex in nearly a month. And that was the whole point.

Friday night, I showed up at her door wearing pretty much the same clothes I'd bummed around town in all day. I didn't shave. I didn't even comb my hair. I just showed. She answered the door smiling and gesticulating nervously. She glanced at my crotch and told me I looked great. Whatever. I wish I could have said the same for her.

Liz had pinned her hair up into some funky little "do" that seemed to strip 50 points off her IQ. The big glasses were gone and replaced by contacts that made her eyes look beady and bloodshot. She'd applied this dark purple lipstick and had this dusting of blue eye shadow going, that women seem to love, but no male I know finds attractive. In place of the sweater was your garden variety, stringy strapped halter which made her sunken chest look even smaller than it was. In place of the jeans were these tight ass-hugging dark disco slacks. And what contemporary evening ensemble would be complete without those big clumpy, trendy, open-toed platforms that should be out of style before the Fall leaves turn. The studious disguise she'd had going at the library was really sexy. Now, I was taking out some run-of-the-mill chick from an MTV pimple cream commercial. Even the whisper of perfume had become a shout. But I eyed her up and down, and lied, telling her she looked kind of hot.

We had dinner at some trendy fly-by-night Thai place. Spicy Asian gruel is in vogue these days for the upper middle class. Sticking to script, she redundantly praised me for such an "original" suggestion as if I'd invented Thai. I can't even remember what we talked about over dinner. Something about her dad's health, her mother's hobbies, her brother in grad school and some funky spinal injury she'd suffered in an auto accident in junior high. Mostly, she just kept ogling at me with these prolonged stares as if to telepathically try to remind me that this was the "big" second date (wink, wink).

On the way into the theatre, she grabbed my hand and said: "I can't believe how well we get along. I don't usually get along with people this quickly. Especially guys."

Yeah, right.

"My old boyfriend hates Freddie Prinze Jr." she added. I had news for her, but I kept it to myself.

Well we didn't see much of the movie. In fact I'd bet Liz had probably seen the movie already with one of her girlfriends the weekend before, based on her sudden disinterest. After a few glances of Drew Barrymore's lopsided, drug addicted face, and Freddie Prinze Jr.'s sloping, teeny-bopper-killer lips, we started to play.

She didn't stop my hand from sliding into her pants this time, mostly because her fingers were too busy kneading my crotch. This made sharing popcorn feel just a little unsanitary, but that barrier usually collapses inversely with the level of arousal. It was a good thing most of the world had the good sense to stay away from this movie because our action definitely needed a half-empty theatre. I kept asking myself, as Liz's head bobbed up and down, if Pee-wee Herman had been on a date would he still have gotten arrested?

An hour and a half later, when the closing credits finally rolled, Liz hopped up and bolted for the ladies room just as the house lights illuminated the theatre. Based upon our activity, I'm sure some facial resurfacing was in order. In fact, I was very glad I kept on the jeans all day. Khakis would have been embarrassing.

When she emerged from the ladies room, she looked much better than she'd looked all evening. Most of the gunk on her face was gone (the make-up, that is). I also found myself happy that I could smell the cherry flavor again. I'd wondered what had been missing. She grabbed my hand and as we headed for the car, kept bumping up against me trying to make it look like we'd been dating for months. We mashed against the car for a while and then talked about where to go next. I had an idea, but again, she beat me to the punch.

"I found some stuff on Ceausescu, that might help you with your paper if you want to come over for a minute." Liz stated, very business-like.

I almost said "what fucking paper?", but caught myself in the nick of time (not that she wouldn't have pretended not to hear me).

Instead, I said: "Wow. Great!" And we headed for her place.

I almost gagged on the smell of potpourri (otherwise known as "male repellent") that permeated her apartment. But before long, we were laying on the couch, polishing off her box of cheap Chardonnay from the fridge. From there, we picked up where we'd left off during Drew Barrymore's slurred whining.

Liz was really a such a slight, bony little bitch. That squirmy, squiggly little body, pushing and pawing for all it was worth. At first I was afraid I might hurt her. But wouldn't you know, the more I hurt her, the more she enjoyed it. My little librarian was really nothing more than a seriously masochistic little squealer, which explained the broken self-esteem she hid so poorly. So I decided to punish her for faking our relationship, when all she really wanted was to get fucked. I punished her for being so dull and common and predictable. I punished her for the stupid clips in her hair. I punished her for the dumb movie I chose. I basically punished her because I enjoyed punishing her as much as she enjoyed having her scrawny little muscles tortured. She smiled and wept at the same time. It was kind of awesome. A little scary, but awesome.

When it all had played out, Liz staggered into her bedroom, while I started getting dressed to get out of there. She came back out in nothing but a sweatshirt and suddenly had a lot of trouble making eye contact. She tried to smile that perky smile, but while her complexion was flush, the light had gone out of her eyes as she nervously folded her arms.

"Well, you can stay over." she extended the courtesy.

Forget that.

"We really hit it off." she chuckled nervously.

"Yeah." I nodded, jamming my shirt into my pants.

"You're not going to stay?" her eyes grew large and sad.

"I can't." I didn't feel obliged to say much more.

"Oh. Okay." she faked another smile. "I had fun. You're a really good guy."

Oh really? Then what's a "bad" guy like?

"Yeah." I nodded again and kissed her one last time. The faint taste of cherry was tempting, but my work there was done.

So, where's the warmth, you ask? Where's the love? I have no idea. And the good thing was, I didn't care. As I said before, if there really were a God, girls like Liz wouldn't exist. Girls who believe they can whitewash their blatant lack of morals with transparently bogus naiveté? What's the point in sincerity with a girl like that? What's the point in pretending to be "warm and fuzzy"? Like the oiled up actors in a porno movie, she gets what she wants, I get what I want. We both move on.

Still, poor pathetic Liz felt the need to send me an e-mail Sunday afternoon. I almost bought it except for the glaring omission of "God" as her rock. It read as follows:

> *Being a positive person is a lot more fun than being a pain in the ass.*
> *On a positive note I've learned that no matter what happens,*
> *or how bad it seems today, life does go on, and it will be*
> *better tomorrow.*
> *I've learned that you can tell a lot about a person by the way he/she*

handles these three things: a rainy day, lost luggage,
and tangled Christmas tree lights.
I've learned that regardless of your relationship with your parents,
you'll miss them when they're gone from your life.
I've learned that making a "living" is not the same thing as making a
"life."
I've learned that life sometimes gives you a second chance.
I've learned that you shouldn't go through life with a catcher's mitt on
both hands. You need to be able to throw something back.
I've learned that if you pursue happiness, it will elude you. But if you
focus on your family, your friends, the needs of others, your work
and doing the very best you can, happiness will find you.
I've learned that whenever I decide something with an open heart, I
usually make the right decision.
I've learned that even when I have pains, I don't have to be one.
I've learned that every day you should reach out and touch someone
People love that human touch—holding hands, a warm hug,
or just a friendly pat on the back.
I've learned that I still have a lot to learn.
I've learned that you should pass this on to
someone you care about.
I just did.
Sometimes they just need a little something to make them smile.
People will forget what you said. People will forget what you did, but
people will never forget how you made them feel......

love,
Liz

How childishly ludicrous, her Godless "Shangri-La". Move to Wastebasket. Delete.

For a moment I actually thought I was going to get some hypocritical Sunday afternoon sermon from my maid of masochism. Something about "God" showing us the way. But instead, she sends me some empty sentimental tripe, torn from of one of her self-help monthlies. She probably read it ten times before clicking her ruby slippers to make her feel good about herself after it sunk in that she'd done a one-night nasty with *moi*.

Regarding this poem, anybody who can honestly smile after having their luggage lost needs to be punched in the face. I volunteer. And ask the victims of incest how much they "miss" their dead parents. Second chances? Yeah, like the recidivists out on parole. Repeat offenders need to pay and pay and pay again. Catcher's mitts? I got 'em on my hands, my feet and stitched all over my body, just waiting for the suckers who don't own a glove. Focus on family, friends and the needs of others? Who's got time for that crap when satiating my own needs are a big enough pain? Decisions of the heart are always stupid ones. Ask your wallet. Reach out and touch and hug? I'm good for that with the cuties. Otherwise, it serves no purpose unless you know you'll need that person for something later on. Selective bridge burning is an art. And as for not letting someone forget how you made them feel, isn't that their problem? Get over it folks!

I don't believe in God. I don't believe in karma. And while the tooth fairy left a spare coin or two under my pillow when I was younger, I stopped believing in her the day I caught her cheating on my dad. I believe in flesh and blood and gravity and mortality. I believe in knowledge. I believe in luck. I believe in possibilities and probabilities and educated guesses. I believe in losing streaks and winning streaks. And I believe in the long run, everything tends to even out in the end.

What I don't buy is that there's some moral omnipotence judging us by everything that we do. If that were true, then explain Hitler to me. Explain 6 million Jews exterminated for wearing the wrong jewelry. Were those "bad" people who got their genitalia sliced and dissected by German sadists with PhDs? Explain Hollywood to me. An entire town where people get wealthy treating each other like shit while they peddle various degrees of open or implied pornography to the masses. Are those really "good" people becoming millionaires with their poolside coke orgies? And what did that guy in the Salvation Army uniform do wrong to get stuck in the middle of a blizzard every December, while people with their giant boutique bags walk by, too lazy to flip him a nickel?

Forget God. Forget prayers. The easiest way to get what you want is to lie. Men have been getting laid that way for centuries. And women love it! Symbiosis in its purest form. Lawyers redress lying as "strategic ploys". Well life is full of opportunities for strategic ploys. And the best liars maximize their opportunities. Ask any CEO how he got to the top. It wasn't ringing a bell in front of a department store, or praying to the ceiling before beddy-bye. No. The CEO strategically stabbed his colleagues in the back and lied to his clients at just the right times. No one ever expects him to be so despicable. Which is exactly why the ruthless despicables always win.

The world is fully populated with people to take advantage of . They think that we all owe each other some unquantifiable debt of courtesy or good will. As a means to an end there's some truth to that. But if there is no end, then there's simply no point. The odds that there's a Heaven or a Hell are remote. But what I do know is that we all only have a short window of opportunity on this Earth which illness, death or…marriage could slam shut at any moment .

You're only good looking for a short period of time. Women know this better than men. So why should you tie yourself down when your twenties only last…ten years? The worst thing that can happen is on your thirtieth (or worse yet, your fortieth) birthday, you realize that all the women you could have had sex with are now married and pretending to be sweetly devoted, sanctimonious housewives. In the face of all that hypocrisy, a man should, at least, have a fair number of notches on the bedpost so the BS that follows doesn't land him in a padded room. When I see a girl like Liz wearing her white wedding dress, (just before the crows feet and facial lines get too deep) marrying the man she "loves" with his six-figure salary and his wealthy parents, I get a good belly laugh out of having boinked her alter-ego: "the one-night whipping girl".

Now I know that sounds cold. But like those beer commercials tell us, the world is a very "cold" place. Liz was playing the game and she won the prize. But then, after she wakes half the neighborhood with her yipping and yelping, she expected me to act as if this was a special thing. A warm, fuzzy special "poetic" thing. Not love, mind you. Love is for losers. At least that's the latest con running through feminist propaganda circles. In the pursuit of sexual equality, women must learn to "love" as little as men do, yet still treat the altogether, meaningless act like something that doesn't leave them feeling like a spunk receptacle. Stay for breakfast (usually, a really bad breakfast from a liberated modern gal who's earned the right to be a terrible cook). Stay for hugs and kisses and a nifty sunrise chat about the morning news. Stay and see how really fucking bad she can look after three hours of sleep and a quick shower. And let's get together at least once more so as not to stigmatize the evening as the one night stand that it was.

Uh…let's not.

I don't believe in God and I don't believe in bullshit. When a person is acting out of unadulterated selfishness, the least they can do is own up to it. I didn't screw Liz because I felt like "giving". I screwed her because I felt like taking. And no hearts or flowers or poems to the contrary are going to make it anything other than what it was. It feels good to take. A rational mind sees no shame in that. Taking is all any of us have. Why should I string along some false pretense with Liz, when she and I can both move on to someone new? Life is about experiences. And with the finite amount of time allotted to us, we've certainly got to make the most of it, regardless of how someone else "feels".

I did try God for a while. Like everyone on this planet, I wanted to feel like a "good" person that some omniscient force would smile upon for my good deeds. But all I found was that I felt like a guilty person who wasn't free to be himself anymore. Thou shalt not fuck. Thou shalt not bullshit. Thou shalt not smoke dope. Thou shalt not get drunk with your friends on the weekends. Thou shalt not want to ever make a fucking dime without giving some of it away to lazy motherfuckers who'd rather beg than work. Yeah. Thou shalt not live. If I have an itch, I should be allowed to scratch it. If I want to feel happy, I should be allowed to laugh out loud. If I want to blow the money I earn on myself, I shouldn't feel bad because some homeless ex-con who couldn't break his heroin habit wants to make me feel like I owe him a living. Frankly, I keep hearing about God, but he never shows up. And his followers have more excuses for his no-shows, than Hank Williams's road manager.

God works in mysterious ways? I don't watch the X-Files. I watch the news.

When I was going to church, reading the Bible, feeling guilty about every pleasure that put a smile on my face, I was totally miserable. Aside from the total delusion, I was miming through life trying to please invisible forces I could never touch or see. Prayers without answers. Deeds without rewards. What was I thinking? The moment it occurred to me that flesh and blood and bone are all that there is, my clarity of purpose and sense of self became so incredibly vivid. It was an epiphany I wouldn't trade for all the religious repression in the universe: No God = a happier me!

And drugs are part of a full life, regardless of what any religious alcoholic tells you. We now live in an age where even the President can smile and refer to his youthful indiscretions as a badge of honor amongst the commoners. What's legal or illegal is a joke (unless you get busted of course). Our grandparent's generation could slam beer, whiskey and wine until their livers fell out. But pot, acid and coke are unpardonable sins? I'd rather have my buddy, who's been smoking bowls all night, drive me home, than to deal with some grizzled drunken grandpa' jumping the median at 80 miles per hour, because he got bombed on legal booze. Drugs were made to be taken. Trips were made to be…taken. And I refuse to believe that someone who's never dropped acid has led a fuller richer life than me. For those of you who know, you know what I mean.

Unfortunately, people are obsessed with connecting to some cursory, irrational, "goodness" that will make them feel better about their cold, selfish natures. Altruism isn't natural. Self-preservation is. Nobody sane can really give 'til it hurts (unless they're having sex)! And unless you really do believe that there's a God out there who gives a shit, the preservation (and gratification) of self is the only course that makes one ounce of sense. It works for me!

Oh, and regarding Liz's e-mail. I didn't write her back. So she'll call…then she'll come over…and then she'll make up some reason to be my little punching bag for awhile (to avoid that one-night stigma). She'll have her "Shangri-La".

And I'll take pleasure in her pain. Then, some day, I'll drop dead. And after that…whatever.

Amen.

finis

THE FACE OF MY SON

It was two weeks before my thirty-ninth birthday. I was anonymously immersed in my solitude amidst the foraging holiday thralls who thoughtlessly herded about the plaza from shop to indistinguishable shop searching fruitlessly for the right gift for those "loved ones" who would not soon forgive them for doing otherwise.

It was a seasonably cool late afternoon about an hour before the early evening rush ensued. Thanksgiving was behind us all and December was but a few days away. And I was only beginning to consider what gifts, cards and quiet gatherings I would share with my dearest friends during the holiday season.

The streets were lighted with a tactless incohesion of bright bulbs tangled carelessly through the bare branches of urban saplings. There were blue bears, green rabbits, lavender lions and pink dinosaurs, absurdly anthropomorphisized into the likenesses of children, propped longingly against department store windows like pandered pagan orphans excommunicated from some opium addict's nightmare. There were candy canes and wreaths of holly, and silhouettes of deer (or to be more scientifically precise, reindeer), and of course, a thousand iconic images of the Grand Wizard of this secular fool's farce, the swine prince of capricious gluttony, St. Nicholas.

Now before you label me a black-hearted cynic, of which I am only part, or a Scrooge, all of which I am none, or a misanthrope, of which I am partially proud, my truculent observance is not in the least driven by any disdain for the holy season. Indeed, my desire is merely to make point of the fact that as always, in his hollow pursuit of Earthen "joy to the world", mankind vacantly flaunts his specious love for his fellow man, yet forsakes all thoughts for our Lord in Heaven who's nativity he fails to celebrate on the very day he is insistent upon his right to celebrate all else. The bastardization of the Christmas Holy Day has allowed the retail listings on the New York Stock Exchange to usurp the relevance of frankincense, mangers and the birth of Christ. The presents, or should I reverently capitalize "Presents", bulging from Santa's bottomless sacks are much more corporeal and satiating than God's lessons of peace, love faith, sacrifice and humility. After all, we could never teach our children to cuddle a stuffed Jesus under the hearth with nearly the enthusiasm with which he will drool apishly over his grinning, factory-sewn mammal as he learns the rudimentary human virtues of possession, greed and avarice.

But alas, this is a discussion for another time. For I know that I live among yet another faithless and perverse generation of men who'll neither be changed readily by any wisdom in my words or converted by no less than the blinding illumination of truth cascading from Heaven on our prophesied day of judgment.

Instead, I will deliberate on another matter of a deeply personal nature which wandered innocently into the autumn landscape of my solitudinous content. For you see, it was on this eventful and chilling November day that I first saw the face of my son.

My son.

As alien a cadence in the rhythm of my bachelorhood as would be the loud thump of a plucked bass string at a classical recital. Yet there it was. All of a sudden. Like the whisper of a traditional sonnet for which I thought I could have no ear. Or perhaps a song for everyone else to sing and dance to, while offering to me, my cue to sit aside in removed observance of their jubilant mirth.

Like no dream I had ever known, or thought I had ever imagined, he stood right before me. He couldn't have been older than six. The world around his face was an impressionistic swirl of movement and color. But very distinct were his deep brown eyes which were my own, his mouth from my childhood photos, his hairline from my mirror this morning, and the young, quiet, respectful, intelligence with which he casually assessed everything around him...including me.

There were differences as well. Although they were residual to the lines which defined him: His color was a light tan, his hair in large curls, and his nose tapered and narrower than my own. His mother stood beside him, as I recall now. But she was merely an indistinct, colorless hem swinging loosely at the shoulder of my boy in his rich and vivid portrait.

He regarded me passively with a childish air, as if I were merely a fixture from the beginning of his life. This unceremonious recognition of me as his father was almost as startling as my first recognition of him. For it confirmed, with no matter of question, that we were part of each other and belonged together…before…now…and hereafter.

Still, the overriding sensation remained altogether surreal. It was as if I had stepped into another life which was my own, familiar to my sensibilities yet foreign to my recollections. The vague and colorless hem belonged to my wife, I was certain. Though I could not begin to tell you who she was or describe how she looked. And though I knew this was my son, I couldn't even recall his name. And I didn't know his favorite color. And I couldn't remember his first step or his cries as an infant or the smell of his clothes or the play we had shared or the day he learned to walk or to dress or to ask politely. I knew nothing of the boy at all…except what stood before me at that instant. Yet, despite my lapsed knowledge of him, I still knew he was my son, most assuredly.

Then, without abruptness, the gossamer hem of my wife quietly turned him away and he receded into the colors of the landscape. It was as if I were supposed to follow. Or perhaps to catch up with him later. There was simply no emotion at that moment. Just a casual interval in a life I did not lead…with a son I did not have in the reality which returned to me.

I wondered if part of me had in fact followed with them. Followed the hem of my wife and my son with my memories and impressions of them intact. Or rather, had I abandoned him by allowing us to be separated, never to look on him again.

Perhaps, it was merely a shadow from a past I'd failed to conceive. Or an alternate present running concurrently with the temporal tides of this hour. Or a future I would see once more…and remain a part of forever.

All I can say with certainty, is that I thank God almighty for allowing me to see the face of my son. And I pray that in Earth or in Heaven…I will see him again.

finis

TRACY X

I. Woosterite

My memory of my first weekend at Wooster was of me and another African American guy on the football team going to our first college dance.

It was the 1980s and we had just oiled up our jeri curls so that our hair hung from our heads like weeping willow branches. We'd take turns snapping our heads from left to right trying to make that swashing sound Michael Jackson would make with his hair in those music videos. I had bought these pencil thin ties over at the Lee-Harvard shopping center after high school graduation along with this leopard patterned polyester sport coat I had to hide from my parents for three months! I also had these brown and white wing tipped Stacy Adams that I kept shined so good I'd have stabbed any guy who stepped on my feet accidentally or otherwise.

All the black sisters at the party (all two of them) wouldn't leave us alone. We danced to Rick James' "Give it to me Baby", Sugar Hill Gang's "Eighth Wonder" and of course "Billie Jean". These girls were all right and they were great dancers, but I must say they were two of the homeliest looking sisters my friend and I had ever seen. During a dance I'd try to look away for awhile thinking they'd get prettier when I looked back again. But then I'd look back and "yech" they were still ugly. So I'd just snap my curls across my eyes and do a spin and pretend I was with Lisa Lisa from Cult Jam.

Finally, during one of the breaks, I was trying to escape those sisters who had started to get real grabby grabby. (I hate when ugly women start grabbing on you. You feel obliged to react violently otherwise people will think you like them). As I reached into my jacket for my flask, I caught this real preppy looking blonde in faded blue jeans, penny loafers and one of those five hundred dollar cashmere sweaters that let everyone know she had money, eyeing me down something fierce. I gave my buddy one of those Morris Day faces, then sidled across the dance floor and started talking to her.

She said her name was Holly Goldbergstein from Connecticut. She told me she had gone to some all girls prep school in Maine and that this was the first time she had really had a chance to cut loose on her own (and I actually believed her). When the music started up again they played Shalamar's "Night to Remember", a relatively slow jam. Holly was a terrible dancer like a lot of the Wooster "folks" but all I remember was that over-brushed yellow hair, that retainer smile and that expensive sweater she had on. Near the end of the song, I saw those two homely sisters standing next to each other dogging me out. But I didn't care. I had taken my first step toward being a "cool" Woosterite. I didn't get home from Holly's until late the next morning.

II. Holly

Holly and I continued to see each other sporadically throughout that freshman year. Sporadically because, after all, we didn't want to limit each other. She wanted to "see" other people and so did I. Actually, I found that whenever I wanted to "see" her, all I had to do was touch base with her some afternoon and treat her badly, and I knew that was a sure fire way to have her knocking on my door later that evening.

Now remember I said that she claimed to have led this sheltered life up in Connecticut. Yet, to my amazement, she was always introducing me to some new position she'd "heard" of or some new way to get high.

I majored in theater because I thought it was a cool way to get notoriety and meet chicks. But late in that first year, I had been relegated to some menial role in some meaningless play by one of the theater department heads. I was evil for two weeks leading up to opening night and beat Holly frequently. The night of the first performance she gave me something to settle me down. By all accounts, I wound up taking the stage ten minutes early and performing a one man rendition of Hamlet without intermission. To this day, friends tell me that my scene between Hamlet and Ophelia was the most awesome theatrical performance they'd ever witnessed. All I remembered was waking up at some party later that night with a throbbing headache and having people tell me how great I was. When that same theater department head who had wanted me to play a nothing role asked me if I would do the show again, I told her the next time she'd see anything like that from me it would be on Broadway, and that I'd stick to her funky little script from now on. (Knowing I couldn't duplicate that performance in a million years, since I couldn't even remember it).

During the school year, Holly and I took several trips to her parents spring home in Florida. She'd storm into my room, depressed over getting a B+ on some quiz, or whining about the cafeteria food and ask me if I felt like driving to Florida with her. If I wasn't doing a show, I always said "sure". I had more sunny two-week, expense paid vacations on the beach my first year of college, than I could afford even today. Then, when we got back, I'd piss off my friends by getting A's on all my tests. (It was really no problem since most of Wooster's curriculum was geared to making sure all the rich kids passed through without much hassle.)

As I said earlier, little "naive" Holly schooled me in a number of ways early on. But once I got my bearings and began to see how things worked, her little patten leather flats could barely keep up with the pace I began to set!

III. West Indian Woody

Early during freshman year I found that the easiest way to actually meet women while they're sober was to join organizations. I was already on the football team but lots of guys were playing that angle. When I joined the theater department I instantly met an eclectic sampling of campus freaks. There was Marlene the Mute. She'd only speak during rehearsals. The rest of the time she'd walk around campus dressed as a harlequin clown miming strange faces at people. There were two gays we nicknamed Romulus and Remus who alternated being transvestites. And there was Bonnie "Betty Boop" who was having plastic surgery done so she could look, dress and act as much like Betty Boop as humanly possible.

I joined the local radio station as a deejay, but quit over creative differences when I insisted on opening my show with Prince's "Head". I joined the chess club. I joined the international student's club. I even joined the campus rape crisis center as a counselor, the job that probably gave me the most belly laughs. I sent so many stupid co-eds back to their "Conan the Barbarian" boyfriends convincing them that "it's just love, baby" it was pathetic. I think half those girls wound up engaged to their assailants.

Still, something was missing until, one night, Holly and I had another one of our fights. Only this time, she stood up for herself which took me by surprise! (She later apologized and took back all the valid points she had made). So I stormed out to a local bar determined to tie one on. I had just ordered my third drink when some campus cracker walked up to me and started giving me grief about "my kind" dating a nice white girl like Holly. Well, I just went off! I busted a ketchup bottle across his face and then beat him senseless with a wooden stool. As his friends carried him away, this old black brother in his late twenties called me over to his table.

He said his name was West Indian Woody and that he liked the way I handled myself. He told me he could plug me in to some serious campus action. Burglary, grass, stolen cars etc. I was skeptical until he introduced me to some really fine sisters. I mean the baddest sisters I'd seen in months. Finally the allure of the "good life" got the best of me.

The first car I stole was Holly's Mercedes. I remember snickering to myself as she wondered aloud who would do such a thing as we ate pizza with the money I had made from fencing parts from her car. My favorite jobs were those in which I ripped off fraternity and sorority houses. Even as a hoodlum, something in me wanted to "get back" at these candy apple snobs for reasons then, unclear to me.

Holly even helped me case some of the sorority houses when I told her what was up. She loved the thrill and she'd do anything I told her. Holly would pretend to pledge the various sororities and get a full tour of the houses. Then she would come back and draw me a map and I'd hit the place a couple of days later.

West Indian Woody was a genius. He kept inventory of what everyone stole for him in his head. "If the man ain't got no paper, he got no proof." he used to say. Holly thought he was exotic and "so cool", she would say. Although I found she thought this of anyone or anything that didn't remind her of her own vacuum packed New England prep school upbringing.

I was making so much money now I could even afford to buy Holly things, for a change…but I didn't. I knew she was the kind of girl who preferred being used rather than being appreciated. I had watched her dump so-called nice guys who doted on her for that very reason. So I kept taking money and gifts from her as well.

Two-thirds of the way through freshman year, I thought Wooster was heaven on earth. But then, it all came crashing down on me.

IV. Trapped

One thing I learned at Wooster is regardless of race, color, or creed…a big mouth girl is a big mouth girl! Holly hung out down at the campus coffee house a lot and started bragging to some of her friends about how she and I had pulled off these burglaries. To her, it was as if we had been out toilet papering trees or throwing eggs. She didn't realize we were committing CRIMES! Unfortunately, that cracker I had hit with the ketchup bottle's girlfriend overheard Holly and told him about us. As it turned out, he was the Dean's nephew, and before long, the authorities were looking for me.

Meanwhile, West Indian Woody and I had had a falling out over my cut. I had brought in a dozen high school class rings but he said I had only brought in half a dozen. He paid me my money, but when he checked his ledgers, he claimed I had lied to him. I had heard that crossing Woody meant a sure trip to the bottom of Portage Lakes so I decided I had better make myself scarce. I figured Holly and I could drive out to Vegas in her new BMW for a couple weeks until things cooled off. Unfortunately, when I returned to my dorm room, the whole floor was swarming with cops and they found a bunch of John Belushi posters I had stolen for myself along with some greek sweaters and other fraternity junk!

If the trial hadn't been so pathetic, it would have been hilarious. Holly sat between her fat rich father and their high priced attorney. I sat behind them in chains and a bright orange prison jumpsuit (If I had called my dad, I wouldn't have lived to see jail). By this time, I hadn't seen Holly in three weeks. I sometimes wonder whether it was part of their strategy to scapegoat me, because she looked terrible. Her hair was chopped off and frayed. She was extra pale with dark purple circles around her eyes. She was wearing what almost looked like a Catholic school uniform replete with white bobby socks and saddle shoes. She stared into space like some sort of zombie.

According to Holly's attorney, I had hooked her on drugs, stolen her virtue, and turned her to a life of decadence. Now I know how Donald Defreeze felt when he was tried in the media for Patty Hearst's crimes. Now I understand why that brother chose to go down in a hail of gunfire instead of facing "justice" in a bias, racist court system. Anyway, it became apparent that I wasn't even on trial for the burglaries. I was on trial for seeing Holly.

When it was over, I got sentenced to 30 days at the Wayne County Work Farm. Meanwhile, all charges against Holly were dropped if she agreed to spend two weeks in Peachbeigh Hospital to deal with her addictions. Holly was addicted to quaaludes and cocaine, but she had told me she started doing that stuff way back as a freshman at that New England prep school, not at Wooster. Meanwhile I wasn't hooked on anything…I'm pretty sure.

So I told my parents by phone, that I was going to spend part of my summer on tour with our theater group. Fortunately they didn't ask a lot of questions. Ten minutes after my last final of freshman year, I was carted off to the Wayne County Work Farm.

V. Saved?

I give the warden at Wayne County Work Farm credit. He wasn't really a racist. To him, every inmate's name was "boy" regardless of color. If he wasn't Strother Martin's clone, he must have been a close relative.

Still, I thought I was bad enough to turn that place out. As a result I spent my first few days in "the box". Remember, this was the long hot summer of `83. The box was an iron coffin that sat in an asphalt parking lot all day and all night. Needless to say, I got a great tan and lost about 30 pounds, but I definitely didn't look like I'd been on vacation when they dragged my parched, shriveled carcass out of there.

The next day, I decided I'd play it straight and just do my time. That's when this evil troll looking brother approached me in the shower. I got a fork I'd stolen from the cafeteria ready to jab into his face, but he only spoke.

"Look atcha'. Ya' smart! Ya young! But cha' wastin' it all!"

I said "get out my face you chicken eatin', chimpanzee lookin', no hair havin', pot belly hangin', can't get no woman sulkin', prison guard lickin' gorilla in the mist!"

He left.

The next day another brother came up to me and told me that the first brother had hung himself that night. But he also said that I had a gift with words and should use those words to help my people.

"My people?" I said as I applied some extra curl activator to my sizzling scalp.

He snatched the jar out of my hand and said: "You ashamed to have a nappy head?"

I said "Yeah". He agreed, but said that curl activator was one of the white man's poisons. He told me Johnson & Johnson, despite popular belief in the black community, was not owned by Louis and George Johnson of the Brothers Johnson and that curl activator was just another way for the black man to maim himself. I didn't believe him until he took me to the Work Farm kitchen and showed me a can of oven cleaner. He told me to read the canister's ingredients. Then I read the ingredients label on that jar of curl activator. They were identical!

He told me then, that I could learn many such things if I simply listened to the teachings of the Honorable Isaiah Hirrambe. According to this inmate, after Jesus appeared in Utah and started the Mormon Tabernacle Choir, he came to Cleveland and spoke the truth about the racist atrocities imposed on the black man. His messenger, a former East side numbers runner, became Isaiah Hirrambe. When Nazis fled to Cleveland after the second world war and sieged the original Hirrambe Hostel on St. Clair turning it into the Hoffbrau House, Isaiah Hirrambe fled to Wooster and continued his teachings there.

I spent the rest of my free time at the Wayne County Work Farm reading old back issues of canceled black publications this inmate had stored in his cell. Magazines like Players and Black Sports. That inmate told me the Bible wasn't important at this point, but instead I should listen to the "Messenger" himself when I got back to school.

I shaved my head and threw away all my Cleveland Browns stuff. (A team named the Browns, comprised of predominantly black players, owned by a white man was just an extension of the symbol of American slavery). I went home for a short period of time, and found my father had suffered a great indignation at work that scarred our home deeply (the famous watermelon incident.)

I returned to Wooster that Fall for football practice and moved into Hirrambe Hostel determined that I would heighten black awareness at Wooster or die!

VI. Hirrambe Football Hero

When I returned to Wooster in late July for football practice, I was like a dreadnought on a mission from hell. During the mornings and evenings, as a new member of Hirrambe Hostel, I was assigned to paint the building from top to bottom inside and out. During the days, I was always at football practice.

Some of my white "teammates" greeted me that first day of practice and teased me about my new shortened hair cut. I just glared at them and they left me alone. On the practice field, it was same old sorry Wooster. They could lose like nobody's business on game day, but during practice, they could sure stick it to the "nigger". After one drill in particular, I remember hearing the whistle blow for us to stop. Then, a second later, some cracker leg whipped me to the ground. I got up and he said "sorry". Then I watched him go back to the huddle and start laughing with his other buddies. I recall being so angry I almost blacked out with rage. My teeth were clenched and drool ran down the side of my face. I was determined to make him pay. On the next play, his offensive squad ran off tackle. There was a pile up and the whistle blew. I saw that ofay standing next to the pile so I started running as fast as I could, lowered my helmet and flew right into his knee. I remember hearing this sickening snap, crackle and popping sound as he yelped like a wounded dog. When I got up, he lay on the ground shivering and convulsing like he had epilepsy. His ankle was twisted backward and his leg bone protruded three inches out of the side of his sock. My coach grabbed me by the shoulder and asked what the hell was wrong with me. I just said I thought I saw a fumble and jerked away. His buddies weren't laughing anymore. A week later, our coach came up to me and told me my "teammate" might lose his leg. I said to the coach "What profiteth a man by gaining his leg if he loseth his soul?" I left him standing there dumbfounded.

Because our league was predominantly white it helped me have my best season. Every time I saw a white running back, quarterback or receiver and realized that some brother should be playing in his place it just made me berserk. I remember one game during pregame warm-ups, I saw this freshman brother on Mountain Union's team standing on the side while this cracker half-back took all the reps with the first team. I walked up to him and said "don't worry brother! You're gonna play today." He told me he hadn't touched the ball in weeks. I said "either you'll play, or the coach will have to come out here and play, himself!" That brother looked at me like I was crazy. But half way through the first quarter, he saw what I meant! On Mountain Union's first play, they tried to run a sweep with that starting halfback they liked, to my side. I beat my blocker, grabbed that halfback by the face mask and road him into the sideline, past his teammates, over the bench, and into the fence. He just laid there motionless with a big stain in his pants. Then Mountain Union trotted another white halfback onto the field. They ran a draw play, and I just crashed in and grabbed that runner's leg and twisted it around like Lawrence Taylor did Joe Theismann until I heard a loud snap! Then I saw Union's coach wince, and reluctantly call that brother into the game. As he jogged in, he looked at me with a big smile on his face. We wound up losing the game, as that brother was quite exceptional and ended up getting 250 yards rushing with four TDs. But the important thing was that I had made my point with my real teammates: The black man.

That year I was all-league, averaging twenty tackles a game. I also led the league in penalties averaging three personal fouls a game. It was the most satisfying feeling I'd ever had playing the game of football. The Honorable Isaiah Hirrambe was pleased.

VII. Hirrambe Activist

It seems crazy now, but meeting Isaiah Hirrambe for the first time was a truly moving experience. I remember climbing those steps up to his room with tears running down my face, awed by this wondrous moment. When I entered his room for the first time, I saw the great mural painted along the wall. It was a painting of Jim Brown in his Browns uniform carrying a sack of money with female tacklers in mini-skirts trying to bring him down. He was stiff-arming one of the tacklers over a balcony railing while the others clawed at his uniform. I later learned that this was in keeping with Isaiah Hirrambe's teaching that women were like wheat, to be harvested and consumed in great abundance, but should never be allowed to be the source of a man's downfall.

While I admired the great mural, the little man in the embroidered "Free Angela Davis" fez turned to greet me. I was so taken aback by this kind, gentle little man. I had been a jeri curl wearer, a moonwalker, and a thief. Yet this honorable leader of men was taking me into his flock. He took a pitcher of milk, filled up a glass and handed it to me. "If you offer a man this, he will drink it." he said to me. Then he filled another glass and poured some Hershey's syrup into it and stirred the milk until it became deep, rich chocolate. "But if you give them a choice, this is what they will drink!". I took this lesson to heart as I began my work.

The first thing I noticed, was that while Hirrambe's cause was just, its numbers were thin. There were lots of negroes roaming around on campus, but they had never thought to join Hirrambe (probably believing the Wooster propaganda that said we were a militant group). This bothered me greatly because these step-n-fetch-it negroes were denying themselves a wonderful opportunity to bond spiritually with their own. Therefore, when I was offered the opportunity to speak at the annual Wooster organizations kickoff rally in Wooster Arena, I seized the opportunity to say what I felt. Ironically, I was asked to speak right after some blue-blood pseudo aristocratic ofay had made the statement that all races were welcomed to join the All Nations Club (which was usually made up of all whites pretending to represent other nations.). This just angered me to the point that when I stepped up to the podium, I didn't pull punches:

> "I can't believe what a bunch of suckers some of you so-called negroes I see in the audience are. You let these people trick you into joining their white supremacist organizations just so they can water you down! They tell you you're integrating! When in fact, as soon as you try to make a suggestion they tune you out! When you try to take control, they tell you you're being pushy! And when it comes time to take the group photo, they stand you on the end like you got there late like the nigga' they think you're supposed to be! And when they publish that photo, they crop it in such a way where you aren't even in the picture at all! Well let me tell you something: When you join these campus Ku Klux Klan organizations, you aren't in the picture! You aren't even out of focus! You're like a pencil or a paper clip or some other usable office supply that winds up in the garbage at the end of the day! Why you lip hanging, Uncle Tomming negroes are nothing but black coal paper weights! You're like a coffee ground that snuck into the creamer! They just pluck your brown ass right out! Nawwww! They tell you you're making

a contribution when they let you run the copying machine or stand on the corner handing out leaflets! Well my brothers you're being misled! You're being conned! You're being took! You're being…hoodwinked! Bamboozled! The Honorable Isaiah Hirrambe teaches us that the only way the black man will ever know justice at Wooster is through complete and total separation of the races! Come join us and learn the truth!"

That crowd sat there in stunned silence as I walked out of the auditorium. However, I'll tell you right then and there, Hirrambe Hostel gained new found respect. And recruitment increased a hundred fold!

VIII. Hirrambe's Guest Speakers

The first speaker who came to Wooster and really made an impression on me was Stokely Carmichael. If I hadn't already been thrust into the movement of black awareness, his presence would have done it! The only drawback with his appearance was that a lot of the white Woosterites invited their parents down thinking it was supposed to be Hoagy Carmichael! You can imagine how those stiff starched parents felt about sitting in on a two hour discussion about African American disenfranchisement when they had planned to listen to some Lawrence Welk style music.

Anyway, after that, I asked Isaiah Hirrambe if I could be in charge of bringing celebrities to campus because this type of thing seem to be giving us good publicity and spreading awareness even among the white students. He gave me his blessing.

I enjoyed making the phone calls around the country to various celebrity agents trying get speakers to come down. However, the one incident that sticks in my mind was when I talked to James Earl Jones! Up to that point, I thought he was a really together man (in spite of his appearance in the Exorcist II). But he got on the phone and talked down to me and then said he didn't speak anywhere for less than $10,000! I told him that Carl Stokes, the first African American mayor of a major city, had spoken for a tenth of that. He said that Carl Stokes never worked in Hollywood. I told him I must have misunderstood his role in the film "The Great White Hope" because negroes like him must themselves, BE the great white hope! I said: "Any so-called black man that would charge his own brothers $10,000 for a non-profit speaking engagement is a sell-out! And not only are you a sell-out Mr. Jones, but you're a traitor to your race!". And I slammed down the phone.

He called back groveling a few days later and said he would speak for $2,000. I told him that I had already booked Huey Newton and Bobby Seale for that price and that if he really wanted to further his cause I could give him the number of the Wooster chapter of the KKK.

Newton and Seale were wonderful! Although it turned out that Isaiah Hirrambe owed them a lot money from some previous dealings that required him to be absent during their visit. They gave us the idea to start the Hirrambe Rifle Club. Unfortunately, the dean's office would not provide funding.

The first indication that I got that there was something wrong at Hirrambe was when Alex Haley came down. I was a big fan of his work and had the opportunity to spend some time talking to him. Unfortunately, my understanding of history and his differed somewhat. The Honorable Isaiah Hirrambe had stated that Marcus Garvey had been elected President in 1924, but that the government deported him before he could take office. Mr. Haley said he had heard no such thing. The Honorable Isaiah Hirrambe had stated that George Washington Carver split the atom first, in his garage, but that white scientists broke into his house and held his family captive until he gave them his notes. Mr. Haley, again, indicated no prior knowledge of these events as they had been relayed to me.

Respecting Mr. Haley as I did, for the first time I had some doubts regarding all that I had been taught during that Sophomore year.

IX. Eddie Duckworth III

Recruiting was always fun. Opening up the minds of young men to the teachings of the Honorable Isaiah Hirrambe was always thrilling. You never knew what directions those teachings would send a young brother. Such was the case of Eddie Duckworth III.

I had seen Eddie around campus for months, but never with anyone of his own kind. He was one of those, what I called then, Shaker Heights house niggas, who, like the family dog who thought he was human, figured that if he hung around whites long enough, he too would become white. He had this ugly little red-headed freckle faced debutante girl-friend who would parade him around campus like a pet gorilla. He had no clue that he was just a sideshow in her little world of show and tell. Then he met me.

Me and some of my constituents were sitting around Mom's Truck Stop when he came toddling in wearing his Izod sweater and penny loafers. "I said you must be mistaken brother. They don't serve no Oreo cookies here."

Right away he got all huffy and asked us when were we going to learn to "integrate" like he had.

"The only thing I like integrated…is my pizza." I said pointing to the white cheese, then the brown sausage on my plate.

Then he went off into some tangent about how good his white friends were and how he and his white girlfriend were going to marry each other when they graduated.

I said: "If you want to learn the truth, my brother, let that little animal trainer girlfriend of yours get knocked up. Now if you were white, she'd probably break her neck dragging your butt to the altar. But bein' the tar-faced skillet head that you are, the only place she's gonna' drag your sorry ass is the abortion clinic!"

Well, he got all indignant and stomped out of there that evening. But wouldn't you know six months later I heard that he had been sent to the Wayne County Work Farm for smacking his precious girlfriend silly when he found out she had had three abortions during the two years they had been dating. And to make matters worse, she had also confessed to having a fiancé at Cornell Law school the whole time!

When Eddie got out of the Work Farm, he came straight to Hirrambe and became one of our most militant and doggish brothers. As I'm now ashamed to admit, under my tutelage he also became one of the meanest, cruelest "harvesters" of females we had ever seen.

Eddie would make two and three dates for the same night and then either stand all of them up or watch them fight amongst each other over him. And many a night the Wayne County sheriff would come looking for Eddie because some girl claimed he had torn her clothes or pushed her out of a moving car…or both!

Eddie eventually dropped out of Wooster altogether. Where he ended up I can't really say. And whether he wound up better or worse off because of his Hirrambe experience honestly remains a mystery. I just keep watching the news expecting to see his face again, anytime soon.

X. Hirrambe Power

At Hirrambe's height I can honestly say that we felt invincible. Even a number of white students became thoroughly intrigued by our presence. Unfortunately, the Honorable Isaiah Hirrambe believed that allowing whites to get too close to our organization would dilute our purpose. In his words: "The color gray is derived from the mixing of white and black. When you have black, you have certain good. When you have white, you have certain evil. But when you have gray, you have nothing but uncertainty. Note that the color of uncertainty is the color of the sidewalks. We must not allow ourselves to ever become sidewalks or we shall forever become trod upon."

With this in mind, I remember being approached by a certain white girl as I stalked to one of my classes with my friend, Ed Ridley. She said she had been reading our paper, Hirrambe Speaks, for the last year and a half and understood our cause. She said she wasn't a prejudiced person and wondered if there was anything good people who weren't black could do to help. I stopped in my tracks and angrily clenched my fist. Such disgusting displays of condescending, lily white, sweet polly-pure-breadism made me ill. People like her, I felt then, were the kind of guilt ridden Keebler Club crackers who tried to salve their guilty consciences by devoting a fraction of their leisure time to some novel cause. She looked at us as if we were bloat-bellied children from some UNICEF or CARE commercial begging for lice infested gruel, rather than men striving for their God given right to equality. I glared at her, barely resisting the urge to pimp-smack her right in the middle of the campus green. Finally, behind gritted teeth, I just sneered and said "Nothing". She just stood there blinking back tears like some five year old who'd been told she couldn't join the circus as I turned and strode away. Ironically, this same girl would later become a friend and co-worker of mine.

Unfortunately, Ed, who had always been a closet integrationist at heart stayed behind and consoled the little snot-nosed, wispy ofay. Since Ed was a great piano player and singer, she talked him into appearing in a show at the coffee house where she and some of her friends were also going to appear.

When Ed told me what he was going to do, I told him he was a fool! I told him they'd have him doing Bojangles soft shoe routines and singing Zippity Doo Da like Uncle Remus by the end of the night. But he wouldn't listen.

The night of that show, we had booked my friend Tyrone, a now wealthy and famous L.A. saxophonist, at the Wooster ballroom to a packed house. Tyrone was breathing new life into Grover Washington's Winelight, when one of the young freshman brothers burst in and told us Ed was being humiliated at the Coffee House.

Me and about eight or ten Hirrambe brothers took up our Louisville Sluggers and headed over to the Coffee House. When we walked in, Ed was sitting at the piano in minstrel make-up (he later explained that they had told him it was 1890's night) singing at the top of his lungs while all the little preppy Woosterites yapped through his performance like he was a bad lounge act. That girl who had invited Ed was herself, standing with her back to the stage soaking up praise from her friends about her own singing earlier. As Ed was easily the most talented musician in the room, this left me incensed.

With one swing, I split a table in half with my baseball bat. That got everyone's attention. Then I walked over to the stage and told Ed to wipe his face off and start his set over again. My brothers and I stationed ourselves along the walls of the coffee house holding our Louisville sluggers like Marines holding their rifles at attention. Ed played for about forty-five minutes and no one said a word or even got up to go to the bathroom. When he was done, Ed got a standing ovation, which we encouraged, as we escorted him out of the front door. We took his cut right out of the cash register without any resistance from the Woosterites. To my recollection, Ed never returned to the coffee house again. Not even for danish and mocha.

XI. Silenced

In late fall of senior year, things began to unravel. Rumors began cropping up that the Honorable Isaiah Hirrambe was siphoning school funds granted to Hirrambe Hostel to support his alleged common law wife, a fat Polish woman, on Cleveland's near west side. I did all that I could to refute those rumors, but some sophomore news hound for the school paper continued to write disparaging articles claiming he had proof.

Meanwhile jealousy within Hirrambe Hostel itself, began to surface. As a star football player and stage performer as well as a highly regarded public speaker, I easily became the most popular and recognizable member of Hirrambe. I didn't realize it at the time, but some of my brothers just couldn't deal with all the press I was getting. In fact, I didn't notice until just before the end, that while I had quadrupled membership, led protest rallies, organized campus functions and been instrumental in building a black student network for Hirrambe across the country, my name never appeared in Hirrambe Speaks, our organizational newspaper. The growing animosity was confirmed when I overheard one of my brothers tell Isaiah Hirrambe that I thought I was Hirrambe Hostel!

This all came to a head in December when Wooster College held its annual John Lennon memorial in memory of the former Beatle being slain in 1981. Isaiah Hirrambe ordered all of us not to comment on the event since we had chosen not to partake in the festivities. However, one night, after my one man performance of Crispus Attucks, a number of newspeople cornered me and asked me what I thought of John Lennon.

I said "Like Elvis Presley, Janis Joplin and Jim Morrison, John Lennon was just another carpet bagging cultural pillager of an Afro-American innovation.

Rock and roll was born of music known as the blues. And no people have ever had the blues in this country like the black man. As long as creative geniuses like Chuck Berry, Ruth Brown and Fats Domino were creating rock music it was considered a 'jigger boo' taboo. But as soon as heroin addict mannequins like Elvis and John Lennon started playing it, then it became all right! It became ya'lls music. Crackers like Bill Haley and Carl Perkins even conned you into believing that rock was just souped up country music. They never told you about all the years they spent sneaking into black nightclubs like communist spies trying to bleach the black man's formula for success into white packaging so that racist America would accept it as his own. Unfortunately for racist America, the power of the black man's music became too powerful for the drugged out pop icons who tried to master it. In spite of their wealth, the music has clung to these icon's throats like a Sudanese curse choking them into suicidal submission. Look at Bob Dylan! He's a rich, famous, babbling imbecile who doesn't even know where he is half the time anymore! If that isn't a curse what is? And John Lennon's psyche-delic acid trip music, a corruption of the black man's original intent, only served to drive one of his followers into madness and deliver the instrument of Mr. Lennon's own destruction! The white men who stole rock music are pigeons of their own greed. As far as I'm concerned, its a case of the pigeons eating the rat poison. And as an old city kid, seeing dirty pigeons die from rat poisoning never made me sad. In fact it makes me glad!"

Well, the next day in the Wooster newspapers, the headline said that I called John Lennon a dirty pigeon who died from rat poisoning. And while that was fig-uratively what I meant, Isaiah Hirrambe was not pleased. He said that both black and white people liked John Lennon and that I had made things difficult for Hir-rambe Hostel. As a result, he silenced me for ninety days. I was shocked at this since I had said and done much stronger things in Hirrambe's behalf without reprisal. Nonetheless, I accepted his decision.

XII. Booted

While suspended, the story about Isaiah Hirrambe's common law wife broke in the Wooster College newspaper. Publicly, Isaiah Hirrambe denied the story as a student ploy designed to disgrace and discredit Hirrambe Hostel. Privately, how-ever, many of us were skeptical at best.

Since I was barred from partaking in any Hirrambe functions, I decided to drive up to Cleveland and find out for myself.

According to the newspaper article Francesca Pawlikowski lived in a small one story house on Cleveland's dirty near west side. She wasn't hard to find.

The house was one of those amazing low cost structures constructed of more aluminum than wood. The kind of house proudly inhabited by poor white trash too proud to live in a trailer park. It leaned against a driveway fence where sat a rusty lime green 1972 Ford Marquis. Everything was coated with a thin layer of soot. Three fat yellow skinned, sandy haired teenage kids of undetermined gender played with a red hard plastic miniature football on the weed laden front lawn.

Stepping over a rusty tricycle half submerged in the dried vines of an abandoned flower bed, I rang the door bell that dangled from two wires sticking out of the door frame. From inside I heard a large animal howl and begin bounding about rattling the windows and foundation. Then I heard a loud woman's voice and two whipping belt lashes and after a bestial whimper all fell silent again. In another moment, the front door creaked open, and a tall, double chinned, wart faced, obese blonde woman in her fifties wearing one of those plaid Woolworth circus tent house dresses filled the doorway with a cigarette hanging from her thin chapped lips.

My first inclination was to run, but I could hear whatever animal it was restlessly hop out the back door dragging its heavy chain on the driveway and realized it would probably outrace me to my car. Instead I identified myself as a follower and student of Isaiah Hirrambe. The big fat lady blew a cloud of smoke into the air and laughed a guttural laugh that would have chilled the crustiest Lake Erie longshoreman and invited me in.

She offered me a seat and I looked for somewhere clean to sit as I watched roaches scatter under the furniture. Finally I settled on the edge of a cracked vinyl chair where a couple of clean spots of yellow foam poked out. She offered me a pierogi from a chipped grease stained plate from which she had obviously devoured a number. I declined. Then she offered me a beer, and disdaining a dirty infected glass, I accepted an unopened can and stuck it in my coat pocket. With that, she melted her pasty bulk onto a dirty pastel couch, sunken where she most often sat, and asked me what I wanted.

I showed her a picture of the Honorable Isaiah Hirrambe in his "Free Angela Davis" fez. She immediately began cackling saying "That's my Wilfred!"

She went on to relate to me that Isaiah Hirrambe or Wilfred as she called him, met her while she was working as a cocktail waitress in a west side strip bar in the early seventies. He had this weakness for pale, hefty blondes, but she was the only one that would give "the little black guy" the time of day. One evening, he came in and showed her two tickets to a Funkadelics concert and she decided to go out with him. After the concert, they celebrated in the back of that old Marquis with some reefer and a half gallon of Mogan David. She didn't see him for weeks after that, but when she found out she was pregnant, she told him and they decided to start dating. She said he was a really sweet guy. He never let her pregnancy stand in the way of them going out bowling, getting really drunk at some bar and going back to her apartment for intimacy. When the first baby was born, he bought her this house and told her no woman of his should have to work and gave her the name of someone he knew at the County Welfare office. They had two more children but never decided to marry because he felt that would cut into her ADC. So they just lived together until he moved to Wooster several years ago.

"He's a really great guy." she said swilling her third beer in ten minutes. "He still takes the kids to Indians games, buys me beer and jewelry, and makes me feel like a lady."

Unable to take much more I looked at my watch (actually my bare wrist) and told her I had to go. But before I left, she said if I had any doubts she had a tattoo to show me. Before I could look away, she hiked her dress-tent up to her massive blue-veined thighs and revealed a wrinkly tattoo with the likeness of herself and...Wilfred, the Honorable Isaiah Hirrambe.

Sick to my stomach, I staggered out of the house ran past her dirty, overweight kids and juked the giant mongrel animal that chased me to my car. I peeled rubber, kicking broken glass up in the air and burned a path straight back to Wooster.

Sadly, I confirmed the newspaper story to my brothers but learned that they had already voted me out of Hirrambe because they had learned of my visit. Apparently, Francesca phoned Isaiah Hirrambe wanting to know who the nice young man who had visited her and bolted so suddenly was. I then told that sophomore news hound that he was right and he printed the story. During that time, I was a man on an island at Wooster. A leader without a land.

XIII. Pilgrimage to the Library

At some point in every Wooster College student's career, everyone should eventually go to the library. Up to this point, I had always avoided the library for one reason or another. My freshman year, I was just too much of a "cool" Woosterite hipster to be wasting my time in a building full of books. My next two and a half years, as a Hirrambe Hostel minister, it would have been a violation of my oath of racial and spiritual purity to allow my mind to be polluted within the walls of an edifice erected in tribute to the white man's published legacy of historical and literary propaganda.

However, at this point, being banished, I no longer had access to Isaiah Hirrambe's personal library. This placed my Senior project on African American history in jeopardy. In retrospect, Isaiah Hirrambe's dubious book collection was quite fascinating, consisting of titles I never again saw even in the most exclusive African American book stores. Books like: Jim Brown's *Tales of the Coyote Ugly White Broads; Nat Turner's Lost Memoirs: Chained Like Me;* Wilt Chamberlain's *Ten Thousand Trojans; Black Eye of the FBI* (a black FBI agent's account of the surveillance of Martin Luther King leading to his FBI assassination); *But Was It Dred Scott's Decision?* (the alleged account of Dred Scott's denied request to sail back to Africa on a bamboo raft); *First Man Killed, Last Man Buried: The Crispus Attucks Story;* Frederick Douglas's *Back of the Stagecoach; The Meeting* (a fictional account of a meeting between Nat Turner and Dred Scott); *Pack Your Bags Nigger* by Marcus Garvey; *Afro-Funk Jesus: The Real Deal* by George Clinton; *Over the Underground Railroad: Freedom the Hard Way* by Dred Scott; *Uncle Booker's Cabin* by W.E.B. Dubois; *Royalty Check Rip-off: The Tragedy of Aunt Jemima and Uncle Ben; ThurBad Marshall; Life Below the Rim*(Marvin Barnes' account of how once-immune pro athletes with rap-sheets are unfairly persecuted and convicted for committing crimes once they retire); *Kill Those Funky Slavemasters White Boy* (The John Brown Story); and too many others to recount here.

I tore the plastic wrapping off of the book bag my sister had given me for high school graduation, slung it over my shoulder and began my pilgrimage.

When I entered the library, it was as if the people there spoke a different language than I. Words like "card catalogue" and "computerized cross-reference" were foreign to me. And I noted two Wooster campus security aides tailing me everywhere I went. It took several hours before I was able to ditch them by ducking into the women's bathroom and climbing out a window and into another department. Still, I was really amazed at how helpful all of the scraggly old librarian ladies were. In fact as I looked around, I noted mixed groups of students consisting of black, white, red, and yellow students all working together on various projects as I'd rarely seen before (with the exception of the theater department which was a Mecca unto itself regarding varied forms of social deviance). Here in this hallowed place of knowledge and higher learning all men seemed to be brothers. Nothing like a little integration to try to raise that old GPA for the dreaded real-world résumé.

Still my faith in the library was shaken when I found that its black history section consisted only of books on the civil war and two Martin Luther King biographies written by white authors. The old Hirrambe rage began to seep back into my veins when an elderly man whom I'll refer to as Methuselah, approached me.

Methuselah looked something like a cross between Albert Einstein and drawings of King Lear banished to the forest. He was a hunched over man dressed in a dusty turn-of-the-century three-piece suit that no longer fit properly.

"You don't want anythin' ta' do wit' dat' junk!" he spoke in a voice that cracked like old vinyl. "The real shit's down here!"

He motioned for me to follow him down a back staircase. We kept descending several flights past the boiler room until we came to a large subterranean apartment where Methuselah apparently lived. There was an old tattered cot in the corner and a pot bellied stove in the middle of the room. But what stood out the most were the shelves upon shelves of old newspapers and books containing reams of African-American history.

"After the sixties, the Dean figgered all this black stuff was passé." he said to me with a wink. "So as they dumped the stuff out, I carted it all down here!"

He had handwritten folios by Frederick Douglas, W.E.B. Dubois and Booker T. Washington. He had every copy of "The Liberator", the old abolitionist newspaper from the 19th century. He had a photo journal from one of the old Buffalo soldier platoons as well a handwritten roster by Harriet Tubman of everyone who passed through the Underground railroad. There were autobiographies of every great African American I could think of. Old entertainment films from the 20's and 30's were everywhere as well as news reel footage of some old Marcus Garvey protest rallies.

Here I had struck gold. Here I had found many references where I learned that Isaiah Hirrambe had distorted the facts about African America. Here I had come closer to the truth than I had ever come before!

I returned many times to Methuselah's subterranean warehouse of knowledge! Herein lay the basis for my senior project that I would orchestrate during my final semester at Wooster!

XIV. Wooster Scholar

Putting my Senior project together still had a number of obstacles even though I had uncovered a gold mine in the subterranean depths of the library.

The articles in the Wooster newspaper had forced Isaiah Hirrambe to move out of Hirrambe Hostel. The day he moved out, his common law wife, Francesca, came down to help him move. She had her face all caked up with cheap Gray Drugstore make-up and wore this all leather biker outfit that made her look like Dracula's mother-in-law. As she hauled his luggage out to the lime green `72 Marquis, a gathering of Wooster students hissed and jeered the couple. This was followed by an exchange of obscenities which allegedly resulted in

Francesca mooning the students and spitting mouths full of beer at them. The brothers who remained at Hirrambe were humiliated by this chain of events and subsequently blamed me for everything. They then issued a bounty for my head in the Wooster paper.

In response I had a picture of myself peering out of my apartment window holding a 42 oz. baseball bat in one hand with the caption "Coconut Heads may enter at their own peril" beneath it published in the Wooster paper soon thereafter. This didn't stop those Hirrambe brothers from tossing a Molotov cocktail in my apartment one night, melting some old Paul Robeson 78's I had borrowed from Methuselah.

I started my own organization called the African American Mosque. We used the Wooster Ballroom as our meeting place. A number of brothers from Hirrambe followed me there. I also allowed women to join which had been forbidden by Isaiah Hirrambe. Whites could not join but they were allowed to contribute to the project which was to consist of a performance series which included plays and readings during the first week in May.

I even ran into Holly that semester. I had heard she had transferred to Michigan after we had been arrested 2 ½ years ago, but she had dropped by campus to visit some friends. She had permed and dyed her hair, lost weight and was now going by her middle name of Annie. She said she was majoring in fashion design and had gotten engaged to this wealthy med student. She even said she had kicked most of her drug habits only smoking reefer when her fiancé was out of town. Because of my experience with "Woosterites" none of this surprised me. Although she said she was quite surprised by my own transformation. She said I looked like a professor with my trimmed beard and close cropped hair. She invited me to a party her and her friends were having. In my old days I'd have jumped at the opportunity. But I declined, because I was too busy. That was the last time I ever saw her.

Some say I mellowed during this time since I had eased my stance against integration. I tried to dispel this during my closing address at the end of my project:

"What does the Dean of Wooster call an African American graduate? A nigger, that's what he calls you! Just because he let you visit his backyard for a few years doesn't mean he's ready to welcome you into his home! And as we leave this college a little older and a little wiser, now is not the time for complacency. Some of you negroes think just cause the man gave you a little piece of paper, the hard part is over. Well I'll tell you I know more mail carryin', truck drivin', retail hustlin', burger flippin' negroes with so-called degrees than any other kind. You go to these employers with your piece of paper askin' for a hand out, he'll still hand you a broom or a mop or a rag and take it back if you don't smile fast enough when he does it to you! I know some of you graduatin' conquer-the-world negroes don't like what I'm saying, but I'm not the kind of man to tell you what you want to hear! You still got to hustle! That's life! No thing comes to those who sit and wait! They got quotas out there. You can walk in looking like Arthur Ashe, but if Buckwheat walks in behind you with naps sittin' on top of his head and a big white toothy grin, they'll hire him just cause he knows when to say 'Yes'm' and 'O tay'! And if that happens, you don't stop trying. Cause any firm that hires a grinnin' bow-and-scrape nigga' like that isn't good enough for you anyway. There's too many intelligent negroes out here with fine cars and nice houses for you not getting your share of the pie if you work hard enough! Now I'm not saying that all white men are racist although I will say that even the nicest ones are prejudiced, though they just don't know it. What I am saying is that as you wish to be judged as an individual, so too must you judge them as individuals. If a white man treats you with dignity and respect, you treat him with dignity and respect. But if some Neo-nazi redneck in a necktie disses you, then you turn his lights out and close the door! This is America! This is the eighties! And if Jim Crow wants to come out of the closet, then you're morally obligated to send him to the cemetery!"

And I waved my 42 oz. bat in one hand and a diploma in the other as the curtain drew to a close.

Epilogue

by Alex H.

I first met Tracy X during my visit to Wooster College in 1984. At first, I thought he was just another collegiate fringe lunatic what with his jumbled up knowledge of African American history and all. But during my visit, I was forced to spend an inordinate amount of time with him and honestly grew fond of the young man. We sat in Mom's Truck Stop for hours eating french fries, onion rings, drinking Pepsis and talking about the direction African America ought to take in order to achieve true equality. "Man, if I could get every brother who spends his weekends doing the Jordache in nightclubs to take up an AK-47 for his own freedom, I'd show you somethin'!" he'd say to me as he emptied a bottle of ketchup on his basket of fries. I remember him getting particularly defensive when I asked him whether Hirrambe Hostel was a fraternity.

"Hey, I see so many jeri curled niggas with brands on their arms like cattle working in carwashes and kitchens it makes me sick! Even slave owners didn't beat and brand negroes like these so-called fraternities do. The pledges spend a whole semester being pummeled and humiliated just so they can fall behind in their school work, get branded and flunk out at the end of the year. Most of those guys can boast 'I was a Alpha' or 'I was a Q' but they can't even tell you what their major was. Hirrambe brothers work hard, study hard, play hard and dispense with all that foot stompin' steer brandin' nonsense!"

After I left Wooster, I made it a point to stay in touch with Tracy throughout his college career. I remember how upset he was after visiting Isaiah Hirrambe's common law wife. "Sickest, saddest thing you've ever seen." he told me. But I also remember how exhilarated he was when he found those African American archives hidden beneath the Wooster Library.

His senior project went off with only minor hitches. Remaining members of Hirrambe Hostel tried to discredit and vandalize his project spreading propaganda against Tracy X and intimidating students to stay away from the programs. One night in particular, Tracy was getting ready to introduce a performer at the Wooster ballroom when all of a sudden someone in the audience yelled "Get your hand off my six-pack!". A commotion ensued and while the crowd was distracted, three members of Hirrambe ran up to the stage and pelted Tracy with eggs and ripe tomatoes. Tracy fell back over some chairs and lay there for a while. Some say that when he got up, he simply wasn't quite the same after that.

After graduation he left the African-American Mosque in the hands of some underclassmen and returned to Cleveland. There he continued his work as an activist from his apartment on Hampshire in the Coventry district. But then, as he wrote to me, things really began to come apart: "There's this woman who keeps showing up in the darndest places. Every time I go to the record store or out for a bite to eat or over to Case to hear somebody speak I run into her. She's very intelligent, engaging, and fun to talk to. But I tell myself she's distracting me from all of my plans."

Finally Tracy said he had asked this woman out on a date. "Someone's behind this." Tracy told me late one night after his first date. "Those vindictive Hirrambe brothers have steered this woman in my direction to take me away from my projects. It's like she knows everything about what I like before I even say anything. It's scaring the hell out of me!"

A month later I spoke to Tracy on the phone again: "I don't think its just Hirrambe behind this. They have to be getting help from somewhere. Last night, she fixed me the greatest meal I've ever had in my life! All my favorites, better than my mom used to make!". Then I heard the doorbell ring in the background and he said it was her and he had to go.

Tracy began missing speaking engagements even at his own Mosque in Wooster. Every time I'd talk to him, he'd been to the museum or the zoo or Cedar Point or Blossom Music Center or the Metro Parks with his new girl. But never anything connected with the causes he had been so passionate about.

Finally, I heard through the grapevine that Tracy X had gotten married. I didn't attend the wedding, but I did attend a separate service sponsored by the African-American Mosque down at Wooster. Hundreds of mourners from all over Ohio came to the service. Ironically, James Earl Jones came and gave the eulogy:

> "The man you knew as Tracy X is no more. But let us remember him as he was. Some of you say that Tracy was an advocate of violence. But none of you here can name one act of violence Tracy was ever associated with outside the football field or an occasional date gone awry. Tracy stood for scholarship and truth. When he told me I was a traitor to my race, first I was angry. But then I was ashamed because I knew he had been right! If he were here today, I'd apologize and thank him for showing me the error in my arrogance. Tracy X was our black manhood! I only pray that we should soon see his like again and that students like yourselves carry on his fight."

With that James Earl broke down into tears. He later donated the $10,000 he had once demanded to speak at Wooster to Tracy's African-American Mosque.

Meanwhile, Isaiah Hirrambe issued a statement from a commune he was now living in with his common law wife and three children in Lorain County:

> "Tracy X was a hypocrite. I rescued him from a life of decadence when he was dating rich white girls and partying his life away! If he had stayed by my side, he'd still be single! But now he's gotten what he deserves. He's married and there's nothing anyone can do about it!"

A few years later, I went to visit Tracy just to see how he was doing. Maybe to see if there was any of the old spark left. It was a Saturday afternoon and he greeted me at the door in an undershirt, faded jeans and house slippers. We sat down and reminisced for a short while but then he started talking about drywall and plumbing and seeding his lawn and the cost of getting his car fixed. Then one of his daughters started crying and he went upstairs for an hour or so while I sat and watched an episode of Oprah his wife had loaded into the VCR. When he came back down, he said he was late for a meeting at his church, but said we could get together later. I said: "Yeah. Sure." knowing it would be the last time I'd ever see him.

Tracy X was not just a great Wooster student. He was a great leader. Though I've interviewed and met celebrities and dignitaries from all over the world, he was unique and his place in history should not be forgotten. In fact, my hope is to some day convert his story into an ABC mini-series and pay off the liens on my estate. Then people everywhere will come to revere the legend of Tracy X!

finis

ALENA SMILED

It was the first warm Sunday morning of Spring. Actually, not a warm morning. It was 46 degrees Fahrenheit. But Saturday afternoon's temperature had nudged into the lower 70's. And Sunday's forecast promised more of the same. All evidence of the mounds of snow which had been heaped upon our streets for the worst part of 5 months and sculpted into curbside icebergs by the city plows had melted into temperate remission.

The sun was shining brightly. Brighter than summer since the trees had not yet sprouted leaves to provide swaying rows of shade along the sidewalks. It might have been too much sun but that there had been so little of it for so long. As it was, too much sunlight was a welcomed intrusion upon the departure of an overlong winter's gloom.

I entered the coffee shop wondering whether Alena, the pretty young girl I had seen for over a year, but had only begun to converse with would be behind the counter this morning. An entire year, yet only within the last week had we begun to spar playfully about the predictability of my usual selection.

Just a week past, I stepped up to the register as I had done hundreds of times. But before I could utter a syllable, Alena mockingly called out my drink and rung up the total. Having not altogether made up my mind, I teased her about having made up my mind for me which she found playfully amusing. The next time I saw her, she waited for me to order. I, in turn, asked her what I was having. Again, she and her co-workers delighted in the brief moment of mirth and we had found our thread of a rapport.

Alena had worked at the coffee shop for over a year. I remembered the day her loud and brash predecessor introduced her. She was a very clean and pretty girl in her early twenties. Pretty and simple in a manner a gentleman might miss in a crowded venue. There was no pretense or feature which distinguished her. And her youthful indifference to our introduction was not at all inappropriate since her father's friends were surely my age.

A full year of comings and goings passed with nothing between us other than an obligatory "thank you" as she either handed me my change or finished my drink from behind the coffee bar. "Cute", I would think to myself and then dismiss any fantasy or notion with the thought that she's at the turn of life where young women are exploring that carousel of courtships with young men her own age, avoiding anything so serious that it might spoil the unencumberances of youth.

And serious is all I know.

Of course I'd presumed similar misjudgments, in the course of my own youth. One moment I was "too serious" for the women who made my fancy. The next moment, they were quickly engaged, married, and mothered so far down the serious path of life that I could scarcely recognize the fanciful and free young ladies they had once claimed to have been through the lens of an astronomer's telescope. Serious grandmothers, they'll soon be. Yet I today, still "too serious" a bachelor.

This morning, I entered the coffee shop and there was Alena looking so young, simple and pretty as always.

"So what am I having." I asked her with unimaginative playfulness. The morning baritone of my own voice sounded to rattle every cup and utensil behind the bar.

Alena smiled from her station and told me what I was having.

"Well there you have it." I spoke to the woman at the register.

Alena continued to smile, only with a radiance that, for the first time, I could say was beautiful. She looked up at me and I smiled back and she quickly looked away. I stepped away from the register and walked over to the bar area as she prepared my drink. I momentarily pretended to read the newspaper I had brought with me, but decided to take in more of Alena instead.

She glanced up at me, and there it was again. This coy, luminescent smile which struck my heart warmer than the sunlight of a full season of Spring. Her eyes were nervous and embarrassed that I had caught her looking up at me. But she smiled again and I couldn't remember when the shy flirtation of a young woman had earnestly thawed the winter frost which had too long resided in my own bosom.

It was an innocent and wonderful moment measured in seconds. Yet one so rare, I am unlikely forget it for as long as I draw breath.

Then reality rushed in cold and true.

She finished my drink and handed it to me with another cheerful gaze. I told her she would have to get out and enjoy the wonderful weather.

"I will." She answered happily. "This is my last day."

It was like having a surprise week's holiday cancelled just before you could back the auto out of the garage. Cut off the engine. Unpack your luggage. Go back to whatever you were doing.

How does one segue a sudden and unexpected good-bye into an awkward request for a date with a fading acquaintance with whom you have only smiles to build upon? Better gentlemen than me resolved such matters in their late teens. For myself, such romantic transitions remain a mystery.

I said something altogether routine, yet coldly appropriate like "good luck", or some such cowardly exit line. I walked out of the coffee shop and that was the end of it. The last time I would ever see Alena smile…at me.

finis

THESE ARE GOOD
DAYS, PICARD

"These are good days, Picard. Always remember that".

That's what you used to tell me on those quiet weekday evenings when I'd climb up on your chest before you turned over and went to sleep. "These are good days". On cold winter nights with seven inches of snow in the driveway and a pile of monotonous paperwork waiting for you on a desk downtown in the morning, you reminded me that "These are good days".

Good days for us to be healthy and young and full of ideas and thoughts and philosophies and love and God in Heaven. Good days to be able to eat our fill and play whenever we felt like it. Good days to bite your hand when you'd smack me in the face. You always tried to beat me to the punch. But I was Ali. You were only Joe Frazier.

Good days to watch you write. Good days to watch you cook. Good days to watch you exercise. Good days to watch you pray to our Lord in Heaven.

Good days to watch you duck in and out of the room looking all over for me while I'm sitting up in the bookshelf in plain view. Good days to listen to your ranting monologues. Though, face it man, you weren't talking to me. You were talking to yourself. You know darn well I really never cared about religion, race, sex, politics or Cleveland blowing another playoff game!

Good days to run like hell when I'd done something wrong. Good days to make peace because you were always too human to know when to. That's right, I was the peacemaker. You just poured the food.

Good days to sit up in your office window and watch you drive off to work. Good days to welcome you home, assuming I hadn't done something bad. In that case, good luck finding me!.

So, I know you've probably found some way to beat yourself up because I'm gone now. I never understood that about you. Everything can't possibly be your fault. My friend, you were the best boss a cat could ever have. You kept me well. You kept me fed. You kept me safe. You held me lovingly all the way up to those last days when I think we both sensed that things were coming to an end. I'll always remember that you wouldn't let me be sick alone. You came and got me and held me. How many people love anyone enough to do that?

While most pets become part of the furniture, you kept me part of the family. Yeah, I know mom brought me into the family, but you were the one who kept me in the family. You were the one who named me and you were the one who took me in when mom had to let me go. You even gave me a birthdate when I couldn't tell you when my real one was! Right between granddad and mom. That was an honor.

We played...for years! Although I did hate the laser pointer. Untouchable light is BS! I loved the apartment and that long corridor where I'd do my 360 move off the wall. But the house was even more awesome. I loved when the new furniture arrived. A brand new couch to crawl over and under! That was a very good day. And stairs! Lots and lots of stairs! And a yard full of chipmunks and squirrels and buckeyes knocking against the deck.

My friend, there are not meows enough in this universe for me to adequately thank you for the life you gave me. It was more than I deserved. But as God loves us in spite of ourselves, you loved me.

I'm not as much for prayer as you are, but I hope and pray that you find the love and joy in the remainder of your life that you provided for me. My original owners snapped a flea collar around my neck and sent me out into the street either to be hit by a car or bitten by some rabid raccoon. The night I was lost and stuck down in that log 15 years ago could have been my last day on Earth. Instead, it was the beginning of the most wonderful life any cat could ever have imagined. Good days with a loving caring boss who made this orphaned stranger a king.

These are still good days. Always remember that.
I have been and ever shall be your friend. Peace and long life.
Your son, your brother and your best friend…Picard the Cat.

—Ghost Written by Donald I. Templeman

finis

About the Author

Donald Templeman is the author of science fiction/fantasy novels *The Last Champion of Earth* and *The Planet of Mortal Worship*, powerful and imaginative literary works which delve deeply into the failures and triumphs of humanity's relationship with God. He is a student of Christianity who enjoys science fiction, fantasy and horror. His writing incorporates all of these elements to challenge his readers to challenge themselves. He continues to write and reside in his hometown of Shaker Heights, Ohio.

978-0-595-36679-8
0-595-36679-1

Printed in the United States
39418LVS00005B/490-537